The Curse of the Golden Gato

The Schmooney Trilogies

By

Bob Shumaker

1663 LIBERTY DRIVE, SUITE 200
BLOOMINGTON, INDIANA 47403
(800) 839-8640
WWW.AUTHORHOUSE.COM

This book is a work of fiction. People, places, events, and situations are the product of the author's imagination. Any resemblance to actual persons, living or dead, or historical events, is purely coincidental.

© 2005 Robert Shumaker. All Rights Reserved.

No part of this book may be reproduced, stored in a retrieval system, or transmitted by any means without the written permission of the author.

First published by AuthorHouse 10/10/05

ISBN: 1-4208-9152-9 (sc)

Library of Congress Control Number: 2005909118

Printed in the United States of America
Bloomington, Indiana

This book is printed on acid-free paper.

Acknowledgements

A very special thank you to my wife of 28 years, Sharon, and to my daughter of 23 years, Katy, who continue to give me the opportunity to make this happen.

I want to thank my family and all my friends for their continuous support, marvelous suggestions, and helpful ideas over the many years of developing this tale from a simple story into a trilogy.

I want to thank Roxie Kincannon and Carolyn Todd for the gracious use of their Edisto Beach house, which provided me ample space and solitude in order to write this book.

I also want to thank the management and staff at the Western North Carolina Nature Center in Asheville, North Carolina, for kindly sharing their fabulous facility and their immense knowledge.

I want to thank the Kalamazoo Nature Center for their book, *Wild Animal Care and Rehabilitation Manual*, which contains a wealth of knowledge and insight.

A special thank you to Griffin Campbell for his excellent cover art work and continuous support.

A special thank you to my editor, Nancy Machlis Rechtman, who continues to develop my words into something meaningful.

And a special thank you to Kristan Swingle, for without her, this would not have been a reality.

Chapter 1

It was a cool morning in Mountview that late June day, as Uncle Steve and Amy were packing the Suburban. We were taking advantage of an invitation from some of Amy's friends to visit the Western North Carolina Nature Center in Asheville, North Carolina.

Asheville is the home of many exciting things to see. I have seen the Biltmore House. It's a real castle and it was the home of George Vanderbilt. His home had about one hundred rooms, an indoor swimming pool, a bowling alley, horse stables, an elevator, and a dining room so big that all the kids in my class would have had enough room to sit around the table. And, the most amazing thing is that this castle was built about one hundred years ago.

I was sitting on top of my gym bag in my room, looking at a pamphlet that had a picture of the Biltmore House. The pamphlet said:

> Asheville has the highest rainforest in North America. There are over three hundred waterfalls cascading through forests, which are home to a collection of flora and fauna that will take your breath away.

I wondered what flora and fauna were and why someone would want them around if they would take your breath away. I continued reading:

> Once taller than the Alps, North Carolina's granite and greenstone mountains have had about 200 million years to soften into lovely, layered fog-shrouded ranges.

I stopped for a moment and wondered what happened to mountains to make them soft and shrink. I continued reading once again:

> Throughout the region, changes in altitude create great differences in both temperature and rainfall, engendering a lush variety of plant life: A singular paradise. Just what does lie over the horizon? It is amazing what you can get into on a day trip in Asheville.

I was still holding the pamphlet and looking at a beautiful waterfall cascading a long, long way into a pool of clear, bubbling water and I wondered what we 'were going to get into' on a short two-day trip to Asheville. The picture of the waterfall caught the sun shining over the rocks at the top of the mountain, making the water look glassy and unreal.

That was when I heard a demanding voice yelling from downstairs, "Hey Austin, Uncle Steve says you're holding us up!"

That was Katie.

I have heard my little sister say that very same thing many times. First, it was how Dad was getting mad. Then, it was how Mom was getting mad. And now, she was saying how Uncle Steve was getting mad. She had to be making all this up.

I used to jump when I heard that someone was mad at me for not getting ready in time. But enough is enough, I say! I believe that she has been making all this up and it's time to put a stop to it. Uncle Steve probably never said that I was holding him up. It was Katie. She was trying to get me to do something that I didn't want to do. She was just trying to annoy me. That's what little sisters do. Right?

"Austin, we are leaving in five minutes, with you or without you."

I jumped. That was my Uncle Steve. He sounded just like Dad and he was serious. Maybe it wasn't Katie, after all. I picked up my bags and ran to meet them downstairs.

We were taking this trip because Amy was invited to participate in a meeting at the Western North Carolina Nature Center. Nature directors from all the local Nature Centers would be meeting to discuss…stuff. Nature stuff, I guess.

I really didn't know why Amy was going or what she was going to talk about. But she had been asked to go and was looking forward to it. Since she would be there for two days and, since my Uncle Steve liked to stay as close to his girlfriend as he possibly could, and, since he couldn't leave my sister and me all alone, then the only logical answer was for all of us, meaning Uncle Steve, Katie, me, and Sarah (I'll explain about her in a minute), to go with her. Uncle Steve and Amy were just about finished packing and I needed to go out and take my place in the back seat of the Suburban.

We were about to leave.

The trip to Asheville would take a about an hour and a half, according to Amy. I was taking a book that Dr. Dixon had loaned me called *The Legends of the Carolinas*. Dr. Dixon is my friend and also the resident know-it-all in Mountview. I say know-it-all with great respect, because Dr. Dixon knows so much about legends, folklore, our ancestors, history, telepathy, and just about everything. He is also a real nice person and fun to be with.

Dr. Dixon loaned me a book, which had a bunch of old stories that happened around this place over the last one hundred years. These stories became legends. The book didn't include the Schmooney Legend, but then again, not a lot of people knew that one. I had already read several of the most interesting legends in this book. There were stories about ghosts, about magic, about a big town that just disappeared one night, and a story about an ancient gold mine.

This trip was going to be different than our others. Usually, we play games or talk a lot when we travel. But since I wanted to read more of these stories, I wouldn't have time to play Name-That-Animal, which was one of my favorite games. And since we weren't taking the Atlanta route, Katie wouldn't have a chance to show us where Mom had once puked, which she just loved to point out to everyone. So I wasn't sure what everyone else would do, but I was sure they would find something to occupy their time, too.

I said my good-byes to Franklin, who is Uncle Steve's unpredictable cat, and Edison, who is his likeable and very predictable dog. Then I went out the front door and climbed into the back seat right behind Uncle Steve, who was going to be driving the Suburban. Amy was seated next to him in the front and Katie was sitting behind her. Sarah, my very special friend who is a Schmooney, had taken on the form of my pet skunk. She was lying on top of a warm blanket in her cage, which was in the back area next to our luggage. I had packed my Atlanta Hawks bag with all the necessities for an overnight stay. Katie packed her small bag with dolls and doll clothes and probably didn't remember to pack any of her own. Amy and Uncle Steve's dark canvas bag was lying next to the cage. Uncle Steve took the final inventory of bags and was satisfied that we didn't forget anything.

Sarah had been living with the resident skunks at our Nature Museum, so she looked like a skunk - just like the first time that I saw her. But Sarah was not herself these days. She wasn't acting right. She had slowed down a lot, moping around, not being her talkative self. Matter of fact, she wasn't even sending her usual messages; she just seemed to be totally exhausted. This has been going on for several weeks, ever since that adventure with Mr. Pickett's pond. Amy and I had watched her walk become slower and slower. Amy couldn't figure out what was bothering Sarah. She thought that Sarah might have eaten or drank some of the polluted water at Mr. Dewitt Pickett's place, but she later ruled that out. Amy had given her some medicine that seemed to work for a while, but then Sarah fell back into this slow, tired way. Amy was convinced that Sarah was sick. So, another reason we were going to Asheville was that other veterinarians at the Western North Carolina Nature Center could check Sarah out and help figure out what the problem was. This was bothering all of us, but especially me. I wanted her to get healthy again.

I could see Edison's face sadly staring out the window at us. "Yeah, I'll miss you, too," I said to him as we backed out the driveway. Apparently, when Uncle Steve leaves on a trip, which he does from time to time, he either has Amy or one of the other people from the Nature Museum come over and take care of Edison. Edison told me that he doesn't mind us leaving, but he does miss us. "We'll be back soon, buddy," I added, waving goodbye to him as we turned on to the road and headed towards Asheville.

This is probably a good time to bring you up to date on all the things that have happened since the last time I wrote, which was many weeks ago in early June.

The biggest news, which you probably will find the most interesting, is that mean old Mr. Dewitt Pickett was arrested and charged with breaking several laws. He was fined and ordered by the Environmental Protection Agency to clean Lake Minti. That didn't take long. The EPA, as it is called for short, is a federal agency that protects our environment. They had been waiting a long time to find the 'Lake Minti Poisoner,' as Billy Johnson had reported in the *Mountview Press*. When they finally did find Mr. Pickett, they went after him quickly. I don't remember the exact amount of money that he was fined, but according to the paper it was a big number with a whole lot of zeros. The EPA has demanded a full excavation of his pond and disposal of all the chemical drums that were seized when they uncovered his hidden cave in the mountain. That cleanup is supposed to start later this summer. Mr. Pickett is going to be a lot poorer, maybe even bankrupt. The good news is that he won't need money to buy clothes or meals for a while. It seems that he is about to be sent to prison on charges of kidnapping. So, not only is he poorer, but he will be gone for a long time, "up the river."

The big question for us is whatever happened to Mr. Jones and Mr. Smith? No one had seen either of them since that day when they were trapped in the polluted pond. I expected to hear a report that after they got out of the pond the authorities had spotted a trail of green slime last seen heading north…but that didn't happen. So who knows where they are?

Since Mr. Pickett was the main person driving the building project and, since Mr. Pickett won't be driving anything except maybe a license plate making machine, the building project has lost its momentum. I doubt if Mountview will get its new hi-rise building any time soon. What is even more interesting is that the townspeople don't really seem to care. There just aren't that many people who would have that much to gain by having that 'girl with a flat top' here in town. And, since the newspaper stopped running the stories, no one seems to care any more.

So things have really settled down in Mountview. Well, except for maybe the tourists. It seems that there are more people here this summer than any other summer that Uncle Steve can remember. No one's really sure why. But as Dr. Dixon said, "Perhaps the world has finally discovered Mountview."

The cougar remained a mystery.

Those of us who knew that the cougar, or mountain lion, was a real threat have been wondering how it just seemed to vanish. None of us have seen it and there have been no reports of any sightings. Keith Reynolds has been out with his Junior Naturalists Group and none of them have seen the cougar, nor have there been any signs that a cougar has even been around. Uncle Steve believes that the cougar went back into the wilderness. Since the deer population out there has grown so much lately, he thinks that the cougar may have found all the food that it needed. If that's the case, Uncle Steve says we might never see the cougar again. He says if the cougar will leave the people alone, then the people should leave the cougar alone…it's only fair. I agree with him.

I was enjoying thinking about all these things and wasn't paying any attention to where we were. I looked out the window next to Katie and saw a large expanse of sparkling blue water, glistening in the sun.

"What lake is that?" I asked, pointing out the window.

"Haven't you been listening? We've been talking about the lake for the last ten minutes," Katie said, staring at me with her mouth open.

"Well excuse me!" I exclaimed. "I just asked a simple question."

Katie and I have been together for nearly six weeks now.

Since I have been talking about updates, this is a good time to give you the latest update on Katie and me. Katie was given permission to stay up here in Mountview for another four weeks. Can you believe that? I can't. Why me?

See, the original plan - the one that I agreed to - was for Katie to stay four weeks up here in North Carolina and then Mom and Dad would come up here for a brief visit. When they left, they would take Katie back home to Atlanta with them. With that plan, I was going to stay here for another four weeks after they left, which was to be four weeks for me without Katie. That was a good plan.

However, Mom changed things on me.

She decided to stay another two weeks with Grandma Betty in Ft. Lauderdale, which meant that Katie would need to stay another two weeks up here…with me. If you are following all of this, it meant that Mom and Dad would delay their trip up here by two weeks. That also meant that Mom and Dad would have to come back here just two weeks after picking Katie up, to pick me up. That presented them with a problem, because they really didn't want to make that many trips to North Carolina in such a short period of time.

So, you ask, where am I going with all of this? Well, Mom and Dad decided to have Katie stay the entire eight weeks - that means my eight weeks - up here in Mountview with me!

That was bad luck for me but there wasn't much that I could do about it. Actually, when they made this decision, Katie and I were getting along pretty well, so it didn't seem like such a bad thing at the time. But she *is* my little sister and things had changed. It seemed that we both needed a break and it was starting to show.

"That's Lake Toxaway, Austin," Amy said pleasantly.

"OK, that's all I needed to know. Thanks," I said.

"Are you going back to your little world now?" Katie asked as she went back to combing her doll's hair.

"Hey, what's gotten into you?" I exclaimed.

"Whoa, hold on now!" Uncle Steve commanded, looking at us in the rear view mirror. "It's not too late for me to pull over and have you two exchange places with Sarah."

"Oh, yeah - Sarah!" I had forgotten about Sarah. I turned around and looked in her cage. She was just lying there, not saying or doing much of anything. Her breathing was slow; I could tell by the way her stomach was moving up and down. Yesterday, at the Nature Museum, I told her that we were going to Asheville to get her some medicine that would help her get better. I also told her that we would need to keep her in her cage while we were at the Center, and that an animal doctor would be there to help her get well. I had sent her a message as we put her into the cage this morning that we would get her out while we were driving. But I was so lost in thinking about the last few weeks that I had forgotten.

"Uncle Steve, when can we let Sarah out of her cage?" I asked.

"On the other side of this Lake…whatever-its-name-is," he responded with a feeble attempt at humor. "There's a gas station up there on our right. We'll stop and let her out when we get gas."

"Toxaway," I said. "Uncle Steve, it's Lake Toxaway. Gosh, why don't you people listen?" I asked sarcastically, looking directly at Katie.

I think I saw her tongue come out.

I sent Sarah a message, *'Hey, Sarah. How's the view?'*

She sent something back that sounded like, *'What view?'* I didn't get the whole message, but apparently, she needed some more rest this morning so I turned around and opened my book to read about gold mines, but thought about Dr. Dixon instead.

Dr. Dixon has been working with me on a new way of sending messages. For some time now, I have been able to send messages to Sarah and she would send messages to me, you know, sending thoughts without speaking. Dr. Dixon calls that 'telepathy.' I looked up the definition of telepathy, which is 'the direct transference of thought from one person to another without using the usual sensory channels of communication.' And that means, I can 'send' thoughts without speaking. But he and I still have had trouble sending messages to each other. I usually communicate that way only with animals.

Dr. Dixon showed me a way that might help us send messages to each other, which also may help me send messages from bigger distances, which has been a problem, too. This new way is called 'imagery.' Dr. Dixon would go to a room in his house and I would stay in another room. Dr. Dixon took a picture and, while holding that picture in his hand, he transmitted this picture to me by thinking about it. Then, after a period of transmitting, he would come ask me to report all my mental imagery, or the thoughts that I had while he was sending. Then he showed me several pictures, including the one that he was sending. We wanted to see if I could match the picture to what he was sending. Right now, we are at about one success in every twenty tries, which isn't really good. But we continue to try to improve.

Amy saw me reading. "You're really into that book, Austin. What have you discovered lately?"

I was reading about the gold mine. "This is the "Curse of the Golden Gato." It's about a gold mine right around this area that the Spanish explorers found hundreds of years ago but no one has seen it since then."

Amy asked, "What is a Golden Gato? Steve, do you know, what a gato is? Is that a town around here?"

Uncle Steve shrugged. "Search me. I don't know."

I was about to answer when Katie, who was putting some clothes on her red-haired doll, chimed in. "Gato is Spanish for cat."

There was a moment of silence as we all looked at Katie in amazement.

"How did you know that?" I asked.

She looked up. "Gato is Spanish for cat: el gato, the cat. I can count from one to twenty in Spanish. Uno, dos, tres, quatro...."

Somewhere between quatro and siete I lost track of what she was saying.

Amy was commenting about how smart Katie was, and I was thinking that I had been upstaged by my little sister. If she was so smart, I wondered if she knew what flora and fauna were.

The car slowed down and I saw that Uncle Steve was pulling into a gas station. As he got out he asked, "Anyone need to use the bathroom?"

I thought, *to take an el wee-wee*, but I kept that thought to myself.

As we got out of the car, Katie was still counting in Spanish, probably at around eighteen or nineteen by now. Uncle Steve and Amy again congratulated Katie.

Muchas gracias.

I went around to the back of the Suburban and met Amy by the tailgate door. She opened it, then gently unlatched the cage, extending her hands to encourage Sarah to come out. Sarah got up slowly and wobbled out of the cage into Amy's hands where she just plopped down.

Amy and I looked at each other with concern.

'Hey, are you feeling any better?' I sent to Sarah.

Sarah sent, *'I am tired.'*

"What's wrong? Sarah, you still aren't your usual bouncy self," Amy said worriedly, hugging Sarah tenderly.

I know skunks are nocturnal animals, which means that they sleep during the day and go out at night to eat and play around. This actually sounds a lot like my cousin Kelly. Kelly must be a nocturnal animal and we just don't know it. That would explain a lot.

Back to skunks. Skunks are active during the night, which means that they sleep during the day. So it would be natural for a skunk to be slow this time of day. But Sarah isn't really a skunk - she is a Schmooney, and she doesn't usually act this way.

So, something was definitely not right and this really concerned us all.

Chapter 2

Amy gave Sarah a little more water. "Austin, why don't you get back in your seat and I will let you hold Sarah. She needs to be held."

When we got back into the car, Amy handed Sarah to me. Sarah immediately lay down in my lap. Amy handed me the blanket and put it over Sarah. Uncle Steve got back into the car and looked around to make sure we were all there. "Here we go!"

I stroked Sarah's black and white coat as we drove down the road. Her breathing was regular, but she was warmer than usual. So I continued to pet her soft fur to help her feel comfortable and my mind drifted off to think about several other things.

Amy asked, "So, Katie, where did you learn to speak Spanish? I am so impressed."

"In school we learned a little bit," Katie replied. "But up here, Christina is teaching me."

"Christina?" Amy asked in surprise. "Our Christina?"

She was referring to Keith Reynolds' daughter, Christina, who worked with us at the Nature Museum part of the time.

"Yes," Katie responded. "I can count to twenty and I know how to say cat and I can say dog and I can say a whole sentence: El gato esta en el cuarto de bano. That's Spanish for 'The cat is in the bathroom.'"

"Katie, that is so cool," Amy enthused. "Christina has become a good friend of yours, hasn't she?"

"Christina is nice. We have a good time together," Katie agreed.

At the Nature Museum, Katie and I, and sometimes Christina, have certain chores that we must do each day. We started out cleaning cages and pens all the time. That was bad. We always got so dirty. No matter how careful we were, we still got real dirty and stinky. My clothes started to smell just like the animal pens that I was cleaning. I couldn't seem to get away from the smell. It would follow me home. It was in my hair. It was up my nose. It would get up with me in the morning. It was everywhere. The smell was so bad that Uncle Steve wouldn't let me in his house. So I had to take my clothes off on the deck each night after work, wrap a towel around me, and then run to the shower. Well, I didn't take all my clothes off, but enough of them to feel strange running through the house in just my underwear. But we all had to start somewhere and I knew that after a couple of weeks of cleaning cages then we would get to do other things. And we did.

The most fun thing I do is watch the animals get fed. One of these days, I may get to feed them myself. Amy said that maybe next summer I could start by feeding the little ones. That would be cool.

I especially love watching the workers prepare the food for the gray wolves. They have this frozen meat in a big cylinder, about twice the size of a paint can. Then they peel off the outside and take an ax and slice off a hunk of frozen meat. And that is what they give the wolves. It seems that the wolves like to tear off strips of meat and swallow them without chewing; it's natural to them and reminds them of being in the wild.

Katie was getting to know the snakes. I know that's hard to believe - I still have a hard time believing it myself. But she got to hold a corn snake last week and just loved it. That all started when Amy needed to put something in the corn snake's cage. Her name is Cathy by the way. I don't know who comes up with these names – Cathy the snake?

Amy asked Katie if she wouldn't mind holding the snake for a short time. For some reason, Katie agreed. Amy then reached in the cage, picked Cathy up, stroked her tummy and gave her to Katie. Katie nervously held out her hands and Cathy slowly slithered all over Katie's hands and arms.

A corn snake is a constrictor. What that means is the corn snake will wrap around a corn stalk so it can hold on when he or she is climbing. And the constrictor will wrap around a mouse and squeeze it, so that its dinner won't get away. Well, Cathy wrapped herself around Katie's wrist and squeezed as if her arm was a corn stalk. It didn't hurt; she was just holding on. Katie was giggling and petting Cathy's snakeskin and I think they bonded. I expect any day now to see Cathy wearing Barbie clothes and makeup. I have got to tell you, it was really weird to see my little sister holding and petting a snake. I can't stand snakes. How did she do it?

So, after two weeks of constantly cleaning cages and pens, we 'graduated' and now got to do other things like help prepare signs, weed the gardens, and repair cages. Yeah, we still have to clean the cages and pens, but at least we don't have to do it all the time. Amy told me that if I continue to study about animals, I would be allowed to assist with the groups that visit the Center. Amy said that if I keep reading and learning about the animals, I might assist in answering questions about the animals when those groups are touring.

Reading is really important – how else are we going to learn anything?

Since I have been studying animals, I have several favorites. My favorite animals are the skunks, of course, and also the great horned owl. I have been reading about the cougar, the gray wolves, and also squirrels and crows. Crows are amazing and very smart animals. So, I'm really excited about coming to Asheville because I'll get to see a real cougar and real wolves and I expect to learn more about them.

I talked with Keith Reynolds, who runs the Mountview Junior Naturalist Program and, since I am twelve, I can join them this summer. Junior Naturalists get to hike all over the area. They assist in tracking animals and help teach others how to take care of animals. That's another reason that I'm excited about this trip, because that program started in Asheville, and now I'll get to see how they do things at the main Center.

Sarah has been a real help, at least up until she got sick. She and I have talked a lot about her being a Schmooney. She keeps giving me more and more information. Dr. Dixon has been over to the Museum several times and all three of us have had conversations. We continue to work on sending information between the three of us.

Dr. Dixon told me that there are three different ways to communicate telepathically. One way is auditory. I learned that word. That means that I can 'speak' without talking and I am 'heard' without hearing.

Doesn't that sound weird?

The voice is heard in my head, not in my ears. That's how I send - through voices that aren't heard out loud, but heard in my head, silently.

The second way that I mentioned before is through pictures and is called imagery. Some people can send a picture of a thought. I can't do that.

The third way is through the heart, kind of like getting a feeling in your stomach. Dr. Dixon calls it, 'a gut feeling' or a 'gut reaction.' I don't do that either.

Through practice, I have been able to send to Sarah, and occasionally I can send to Dr. Dixon. He and I still can't do that very well. We have tried that at his house several times. Once I was able to 'hear' him from outside his house. I have tried to send him messages while talking out loud, like when Sarah and I started talking, which seems to work the best. We will keep on trying.

I looked down and noticed that Sarah was still fast asleep. I took the blanket and pulled it over her body to keep her warm. She needed her rest. I looked at my open book and thought about what Dr. Dixon had told me about the 'Legend of the Golden Gato.'

It was like I could actually see Dr. Dixon standing in front of me saying, "There is a legend about gold mines in this area, right around Mountview. This is very possibly true since there was a very big gold mine close to here, the Reed Gold Mine, just outside of Charlotte, North Carolina. The first gold rush in the United States occurred in 1799 in Cabarrus County, North Carolina, all started by Conrad John Reed, who was just about your age at the time. Until the discovery of gold at Sutter's Mill California in 1849, North Carolina was the nation's gold-producing state.

"Once the rich strikes in the West occurred, the North Carolina mines were nearly abandoned. Many who had followed the sounds of 'Eureka!' in the western gold fields had practiced their mining skills right here, in this part of the country. Also, the town next to Mountview is named Prospect for a reason.

"So, we know that there is gold in these mountains. Matter of fact, the next time you go to Charlotte, there is the Mint Museum that tells you all about it. You should see it.

"So, I would surmise that the legend about gold is definitely true. But in my research I was unable to find any 'Curse of the Golden Gato,' as you mentioned. Sorry to tell you that this may be one of the many legends that have very little substance.

"Legends are like playing that game telephone - you know, that one we all played as children. We would sit in a circle with anywhere from five to ten children and one child would have a short story whispered in their ear. That child would then whisper the story to the person on their left and then that person would tell the story to the person on their left, and so on and so forth. The story would work its way all around the circle, until it ended up right next to the child that started the story. That's when the fun began, when the child who was the last to hear the story would tell it as they heard it. And after that child finished telling that version, the original story was read. Of course, all the children would laugh because the story never ended up the way it started."

Dr. Dixon cautioned, "Keep that in mind when you read anything that has been passed on from generation to generation. The more generations that the story was passed through would be like adding more children to the circle. So, I am sorry to say, the 'Curse of the Golden Gato' seems to have hit a dead end."

Of course I was sad to hear that. 'Golden Gato' was such a cool name.

Dr. Dixon continued, "At least that's what I thought, because I could not find any more information. But, having done this as long as I have, I decided to roll my sleeves up, as they say, and really get to work. I thought that maybe, just maybe, this legend might be a combination of earlier legends - kind of a hybrid, if you will. Sometimes that happens."

I remember Dr. Dixon taking his glasses off, sitting back in his chair, saying, "It was that way with the legend of Silas Shorter. He lived about one hundred years ago and was thought to be a magician with magical powers who had the ability to tell you how long you would live. Well, we found out that there was no such person named Silas Shorter in this part of the country. However, we did discover that there was a Silas Carpenter who lived in Shortridge, a small town out near Franklin. Well, the only connection that the real Silas had with the spirit world was that he built a still and sold whiskey. And bad whiskey at that. It so happens that his whiskey was so bad that some people died after drinking it. So there was some truth to the legend after all - if you happened to drink Silas Carpenter's whiskey, there was a good chance you would die, and shortly. So I guess, in a way, he could predict your death. You can see how these things can get all mixed up."

Then Dr. Dixon leaned forward to make a point. "Now, getting back to the Golden Gato. I happened to find a legend that could have been the one we hear of today. Gold was on the minds of the Spanish conquistadors as they discovered New World lands for their king. They were looking for gold for their country and anxious to find gold for themselves, too. Sometimes that priority would change.

"Many of the first English adventurers who came to North America were looking to find gold, too. Although there were stories that the Spanish had found gold in this area, the English, as they traveled through and explored the Appalachians, failed to substantiate these rumors. If someone had discovered the gold, that discovery was never officially reported. But that doesn't mean it didn't happen!

"It could have been kept very quiet and, my guess is, it probably was. This blind pursuit of wealth made some people rather ruthless. It was rumored that there was a hidden Appalachian gold mine discovered by a Spaniard named El Capitan Eduardo Zapatero and the mine was marked 'el gato dorado grande.' Loosely translated, that meant a large cat made of gold was presumably standing at the entrance of the mine. Who knows what that would be worth? A lot of money, that's for sure.

"So, for a long time now, people have been looking in the mountains in this area for a large lion made out of gold, marking the entrance to an old, abandoned gold mine. However, it may not have been a large lion made out of gold, as we would think, but a large lion that was golden, or even a tawny cat, or, should I say, a mountain lion.

"The Spanish may have invented the story to scare the locals away and to keep the gold for themselves. Remember, the mountain lion, which was also called the Eastern cougar, had been here for a long time. And remember, that since the mine was supposedly way back up in the wilderness, up high in the mountains, cougars roamed in that area and some may have actually built a home in that gold mine. The truth may have actually been that this mine entrance was guarded by large mountain lions. And, that very well may have also been true. Mountain lions are ferocious and deadly animals, which would have kept everyone away.

"Now, all of that would indicate that there was truly a 'Legend of the Golden Gato.'

Unfortunately, there wasn't anything that I could find regarding the curse though…at least not until I stumbled upon a local paper written way back in 1803. You see, in 1803, there was wild excitement when someone recovered a lump of gold weighing twenty-eight pounds from a place on the northwest side of Little Meadow Creek near Charlotte. Well, that was quite a find and all the gold attention was shifted to the Charlotte area. However, at that very same time, there was a similar gold find north of Prospect.

"Apparently, a prospector carried a lump of heavy yellow metal into his camp. Earlier in the day, he told his partner that he was going to scout for a new claim site. He returned in the afternoon and told his partner a wild tale about finding a 'hole' in the mountain, partially blocked by fallen rocks, and showed him that lump of heavy, yellow metal. He explained that he saw a large, shiny object in this hole in the mountain and, using his pickax, he pried a piece of gold from the large object. He showed it to his partner who later said it was the size of a 'small smoothing iron' and weighed about seven pounds. His partner said there was more and that the object was huge. He didn't want to keep the gold at his site, so he left the next morning to bring it to town for safekeeping.

"Unfortunately, his partner never saw him again…nor did anyone else. He never made it to town. That was the end of the story. Of course, his partner searched the area for years until he finally gave up, having never found the hole in the mountain. Perhaps the 'Golden Gato' cursed the prospector, and he either suffered from an accident on the way into town or, perhaps he was killed by an avenging mountain lion. No one will ever know.

"So, it appears that we have found a story of 'la maldición del gato dorado' and we also have the fact that gold has been mined in this area. So, when you add fact to a story, with a little remote possibility added in, it could add up to a substantiated legend. However, like so many other legends, this one may have taken on a life of its own. So, who knows?

"There are some people who believe this stuff. Of course, there are some people who still believe in Bigfoot, the Loch Ness Monster, and the Tooth Fairy. You aren't thinking that this is true, are you?"

I looked out the window and saw that we were now on the Interstate. The sign said I-26 and we were in Hendersonville, North Carolina. Amy was looking at me. "So, Austin, what about the 'Legend of the Golden Gato?'"

"Oh yeah. Well, there was a big lion made out of gold that guarded the entrance to an old gold mine around the Mountview and Prospect area. No one really knows if it was a big lion statue made out of gold or a big, golden mountain lion that guarded the entrance. But they believe the mine is cursed," I told her.

Uncle Steve said, "Well now, by changing a few words around, someone could be in for one real big disappointment."

"You could either have gold to buy dinner or you could say 'gold-bye' and become dinner," Amy joked.

Uncle Steve was smiling and seemed to enjoy her remark. I thought that it needed some work. Amy went back to her paperwork and Katie was playing with her dolls. The blonde one now had her hair wrapped around her face, like a sack. What was up with that?

I was thinking about what a great summer this had been. I wasn't sure what was going to happen next. I looked down at Sarah, who was covered by the blanket. All I could see was the side of her little head and I noticed that her eyes were closed. She was breathing slowly and peacefully; she seemed to be fine, but I was still concerned.

I wondered if any of the kids back in Atlanta had ever touched the fur of a live skunk. Or if any one of them got to see just how smart a crow is. I wondered if any of them had touched the back of a real live deer…or walked in the woods and listened to all the animals. I don't think that they have had those experiences. Most of my friends spend lots of time playing video games and watching television. Too bad.

Now don't get me wrong. Video games and television are great. But you can't do that all the time. They will take control of your life. All of us should go out and experience what nature is all about. It's all around us. We will be involved with Mother Nature the rest of our entire lives, so why not take some time to understand it?

I smiled. Boy, was I lucky for my experiences. I thought about some more of them. I wondered if any of my friends back in Atlanta ever had a deadly cougar chasing them. Or if any of them have had a real live raccoon jump in their arms.

My smile disappeared as I wondered if they had ever been held hostage and worried about staying alive. Well, now that I think about it, maybe they **could** relate to the hostage thing. At least anyone who has had to suffer through eighth grade English has probably felt like a hostage. Don't you think so?

But the message is this – people have got to give nature a try. They just might like it. It's a whole different world to experience. Just like Wayne Gretzky said, "You will always miss the shots you never take."

I wondered if Mr. Berry had ever used that quote.

Chapter 3

The Suburban was exiting off the Interstate and stopped at the 'red light' like they say in Mountview. Amy put down her papers and turned around while we waited for the light to change. "Austin, we will need to put Sarah back in her cage. Is she OK?"

"I think so, but she isn't talking very much. She seems to be warmer than usual," I responded as I continued to stroke Sarah's fur. "She looks real tired."

As I looked at Sarah, I noticed something odd about her tail. I looked closer and noticed that her tail didn't look like a skunk's tail anymore. Now that I thought about it, I wasn't sure what a skunk's tail looks like. I really hadn't noticed it before, but Sarah's tail was looking weird. "Amy, did Sarah always have a weird tail?"

Amy turned around again. "What do you mean?"

"I don't know what her tail is supposed to look like." I looked down and held Sarah's tail in my hand. "I don't know, but it looks longer than usual and flat. It looks different."

"Austin, I don't think her tail is the problem," Amy observed, before turning back around.

It was like Sarah the skunk was changing back to Sarah the Schmooney. But this time, very, very slowly. I guess it was just my imagination, but something seemed different. Was her tail beginning to look like a beaver's tail? No, no, it couldn't be. It was just my imagination.

"We will need to put her back in her cage before we get to the Center. Steve, would you please pull over someplace soon?" Amy requested.

"Sure," Uncle Steve replied.

"Hey, girl," I said out loud. "Are we getting any better?" I picked Sarah up in my hands and turned her around to see her face.

'Not really,' she sent. *'I'm just hot and tired and sleepy.'*

The Suburban stopped. We got out and placed Sarah back in her cage. Amy gave her some more water to help cool her down. "I may have some time before our meeting. We can get a closer look at her in their laboratory. We'll find out what's wrong with her, don't worry, Austin." Amy patted me on my arm as she closed the door.

We drove up a road that had a long golf course on one side. Golf courses are really beautiful places. I was looking at the thick, green grass, the neatly trimmed bushes, several crystal clear ponds, and precision-cut putting greens with their flags blowing in the breeze, enticing the approaching golfers. I could see a lot of golfers swinging their clubs trying to make contact with the little white balls. Most of them were walking around with smiles on their faces. Golf is a great game that gets you outdoors and helps you relax. Nothing wrong with that. Then I saw a lone figure standing in a sand trap. The sun illuminated his yellow shirt and his chrome-plated club glistened as it swung towards the ground. A cloud of sand erupted high into the air. Apparently, the ball didn't go where the golfer had hoped it would. I could tell instantly. Because the guy threw his club way up in the air.

Oh well, so much for the relaxation of the game of golf. At least he was outdoors.

We turned right onto a bridge that led us over a creek and, after traveling a short distance up a winding road, we entered a parking lot. This must be the place. Uncle Steve stopped the car and we could see the front of the building at the end of the parking lot about one hundred feet away.

"Let's go inside and get acquainted," Amy suggested. "We'll find out where we can take Sarah for observation. Katie, would you mind waiting out here with Sarah until we know where we're taking her?"

Katie shook her head. "No, I don't mind at all." She sat down on the ground next to the Suburban after Uncle Steve took Sarah's cage out.

"Thanks, Katie. We'll be right back," Amy assured her.

As the three of us approached, I saw that the building was made of wooden rustic planks with a natural stone floor. Actually, the whole building looked natural - like it was built from materials from the land. I'm sure they planned it that way.

Amy pointed to a barn off to our right that was at a lower level than we were. "That's part of the Educational Farm. Along with the exotic animals, they also have domesticated animals, which they keep there. Animals like calves, goats and sheep. They have everything here."

The sign in front of us read: *Welcome to the Western North Carolina Nature Center.*

We entered the front door and walked up a flight of stairs. Once at the top of the stairs, I could see a desk, cash register and gift shop in front of me, and on my left there was a weather station exhibit, which looked cool. Amy and Uncle Steve walked over to the receptionist to probably ask for directions or to check in. On the other side of the room, there were offices – they didn't really interest me. I decided to stay out here and enjoy the weather station.

At the weather exhibit there were pictures showing the different formations of clouds. I knew something about clouds. Cumulus clouds were the big puffy ones. Cirrus clouds were the highest. And, there was a picture of a big, dark, powerful thunderhead, called a cumulonimbus. The exhibit showed how people can predict weather just by looking at the clouds. Cool.

Amy walked over to me while Uncle Steve went down the steps. "My meetings start at one o'clock today." She looked at her watch. "So we have about an hour to take a look at Sarah. Steve went to get Sarah and Katie and he'll bring them through the downstairs door to a room down there. Do you want to go hold the door for him? I'll meet you downstairs."

I agreed and went downstairs to open the door for Uncle Steve. "Thank you, sir," he said, carrying Sarah and her cage. Katie made a face at me as she bounced through the door behind them.

All four of us walked through a door leading into a vacant room, then we went through another door. We were now in a very white room with very white walls and several very white tables, some with cages on them. Some very white sinks lined the other wall. I guessed we were now in the 'Observation Room,' which reminded me of the kind of rooms you see in hospitals, especially since the room reeked with the smell of rubbing alcohol.

Uncle Steve carried the cage into the room and placed it on one of the tables. Sarah was motionless, and probably asleep - no cause for alarm. Amy entered the room and had to physically remove Sarah from her cage, gently placing her on a blanket on one of the sterile looking white tables. I was still thinking about the room, looking around and getting dizzy due to the strong alcohol smell, when I noticed Sarah. Something was wrong.

It was her tail!

Her tail had definitely gotten longer. Really! It was not only longer, but now it was becoming flat. A man wearing a white lab coat entered the room from behind us, said hello, and moved next to Amy. I rushed over to Sarah and quickly covered her back and tail with a blanket so that the man wouldn't see it. Amy gave me a puzzled look. I didn't have time to explain so I just smiled.

"So, this is Sarah?" the man asked as he moved towards her.

Please don't lift the blanket, I thought.

"Yes, the one and only Sarah," Amy replied. "She seems to have a bit of a cold or something, and has had it now for several weeks. We have tried several possible remedies, but with little sustained result."

She stopped for a moment and looked at the rest of us. "I'm sorry, this is Ron Baker. Ron is the Animal Curator and Senior Naturalist here at

WNC. Ron, this is Steve, Katie, and this is Austin," she said, motioning to each of us.

"Very nice to meet you all," Mr. Baker smiled.

"Ron and I are going to take a look at Sarah. Since there isn't much for you to do down here, why don't you go enjoy yourselves and look at the Main Exhibition Hall?" Amy suggested. " I'll join you later. There really isn't much you can do here now. Really."

I didn't know what to say. If he looked at Sarah's tail, he would definitely know that something was wrong. He would know that Sarah wasn't what she appeared to be. The legend of the Schmooney would then become public. Things were about to go from bad to worse. I had to do something. But what?

"Uh," I interrupted the momentary silence. "Uh, Amy could I speak to you before we leave? In private, please."

Amy had a puzzled look on her face. "Sure, Austin." She looked at Uncle Steve, then at Mr. Baker. "Why don't we talk out there in the hall?" She pointed towards the door. "We'll be right back."

"Yeah, great, thanks," I said as we moved into the hallway.

Amy looked at me quizzically. "Well?"

"Did you see Sarah's tail? She's changing! Her tail looks like a beaver!" I blurted out in one panicked breath. "What will happen if he, that guy in there, sees her tail? It will be all over. The legend will be public and they will take Sarah away and do tests on her and we'll never see her again and I'm scared."

While I was talking, Amy was trying to get me to settle down. How could I settle down? This was a time to be scared.

"Austin!" Amy commanded sharply. The tone of her voice got my attention. Amy paused to see if the others had heard her. Her voice lowered. "Get a hold of yourself. Now tell me slowly, what is the problem?"

"OK." I looked back into the room. They were all quietly talking and the blanket still covered Sarah. "Sarah's changing back into a Schmooney. Her tail is different. It looks like a beaver tail!"

"Are you sure?" Amy asked.

"Yes, I'm sure!" I looked back into the room. Everyone was still talking quietly. "I saw it in the car and it's even more noticeable now. What are we going to do?" I asked nervously.

"I really don't know." Amy took a deep breath. "Oh, this could be terrible." I could tell her mind was racing. "OK, well it's too late to take Sarah away. So I must keep the blanket on her while Ron checks her out." She spoke softly so the others couldn't hear her.

"OK, this is what we'll do. You and the others will leave us alone with Sarah. I will keep the blanket on her at all times. Ron will just check some of her vitals, no serious examination today. Maybe he'll discover something about her that will help us learn what's wrong with her. But I think I can keep it a secret for today. Tonight we'll keep her down here in this room, so she will be out of the way and no one will see her. Tomorrow morning, I will be here first thing and see if she has changed any further. At that time, we'll have to make a decision. If she needs medical help and, if it means giving away the legend in order to save her life, we must make that decision. Do you understand, Austin? What choice would you make?"

I didn't have to think about the answer. I knew that we had to save her life. So I answered, "Yes, we must save her life - even if it means giving away her identity. We will have to give it up. We can't let her die."

"And we won't. She'll be fine today and tonight. Don't worry. We won't have to make any decisions until tomorrow. So let me handle it today, OK?" Amy asked.

"OK," I agreed. Amy made me feel so much better. I knew that she would do the right thing. I also knew that Amy would save Sarah and get her better soon. I had to keep that in mind - at least until tomorrow.

We went back into the room. Amy patted me on the back. "Austin is concerned about Sarah and we needed to talk about it. Everything will be fine. Ron, let's take a quick look at Sarah and the rest of you, go enjoy the Western North Carolina Nature Center." She looked at me and winked.

Mr. Baker gave us directions and we exited from the back of this building only to have to walk through another door into the next building.

We entered the Main Exhibition Hall, which was really cool. There were a lot of different exhibits. There were tanks of water holding fish, more exhibits with snakes, an amphibian area for frogs, salamanders, and other stuff that I wasn't too sure what they were. In the back, there was a big area, which had a sign that read 'Nocturnal Hall.' I saw that Katie had walked over to the snake exhibit. I think she found her calling!

I approached the salamander exhibit. One sign read 'Eastern Newt' and another sign read 'Northern Red Salamander.' There was also a sign above another tank that read 'Slimy Salamander.' I thought all salamanders were slimy - why did they decide to call this particular one 'Slimy?' Perhaps they ran out of names and 'slimy' was the only name they had left. Or maybe this salamander was the slimiest of all salamanders, so it got the name. Maybe they should rename it 'Slimiest Salamander' - who knows?

I went on looking at the other exhibits. There was one more salamander tank. I looked in it. That was a mistake! Looking into the tank or 'habitat' as they call it, I came face to face with the ugliest, most hideous thing I had *ever* seen.

"What is that?" I asked, pointing at the thing. But I didn't get an answer.

I looked around and Uncle Steve had walked over to the snakes with Katie and didn't hear my question. So I didn't bother him. I looked for a sign or something. There was a sign and it read 'Eastern Hellbender.'

"An Eastern Hellbender?" I whispered in amazement.

This dark brown, slimy animal was about two feet long, with a flat body and a flat head. Real ugly, if you ask me. It had one beady eye on each side of its flat head and it had fleshy folds of skin running down to the sides of its body. The four legs were short and stubby with little toes on each foot. This…thing…had dark blotches all over its body. It should have smelled. It looked like it should stink. But it didn't. After looking at it for a while, I didn't think I would ever get it out of my mind. I shook my head. Nope. It was still in my mind. I doubted that I would ever go to sleep again. Wherever it lived, I hoped I would never have to go there. On to the next exhibit. Goodbye, Eastern Hellbender.

I decided to head towards the sign that read 'Nocturnal Hall. Come On A Walk With Us As We Enter The World Of The Night.' This one was for me.

There was a button under a sign that read 'Auditory Presentation,' so I pushed it. A man's voice started speaking. "In Nocturnal Hall you will find animals that you would not normally see on an afternoon hike in the woods. These are animals that are active at night, foraging the forests. Your first encounter as you enter the world of night will be the Eastern cottontail rabbit and the Southern flying squirrels. The Eastern cottontail can be seen not only in the night hours but also at dawn and dusk. They are the best-known and most widely-distributed rabbit of North America."

I didn't know that rabbits came out at night. I always remember seeing them in the morning and sometimes during the day. I guess I really never thought much about it. The Center kept Nocturnal Hall dark but I was able to see the animals in their habitats because although it was dark, there were soft red lights illuminating the exhibit. Uncle Steve was now standing next to me and I asked him about the lights.

"Red lighting in the exhibit hall allows us to see these animals but is not detected by the animals - they don't see the red light. During our night here in the exhibit hall, the animals think it is day, because when we aren't here, bright lights come on in the exhibit so the animals sleep, because they are nocturnal. When we are here, the red lights come on, instead of the normal bright lights. Animals cannot see the red light so they think it's dark which means it's night to them, which means time to go outside. So when the red lights come on, the animals think it's night and they come out and move around. That is the only way we can get to see these animals, when they think that it's dark out. We're fooling them," he explained.

The man's voice continued. "In the same habitat you will also find the Southern flying squirrel. Many people are unaware of their presence because of their nocturnal activities. The flying squirrel is a very small animal weighing between two and three and one half ounces. The most noticeable feature is the loose fold of skin which extends from the wrists of the forearm to the ankles of the hind legs."

There was a picture of a squirrel in flight. So that's how they fly. Well, not really fly - they kind of glide from tree to tree. It's like having a parachute permanently sewn to your arms. That would be great to have as a shirt or coat. Maybe the airlines could have these and give each person a glide jacket to wear. In case they have an airplane problem, everybody could just jump out of the plane and glide to safety. I will have to call Delta the next time I am in Atlanta and tell them about my idea.

Looking around the room, I saw an amphibian exhibit where there were supposed to be frogs and toads. I looked in and was relieved not to see an Eastern Hellbender. Actually, I couldn't see any frogs or toads, either. They were all gone. Uncle Steve told me that their camouflaged colors are so good, you could be looking right at them and you wouldn't see them. I didn't know if I should believe that. I still think the exhibit was empty.

The voice continued. "Our next inhabitant of Nocturnal Hall is the green heron. Herons are often mistaken for cranes. They can grow to be twenty-two inches tall. When the green heron gets excited, it raises its crest and jerks its tail, which makes the bird look bigger and more frightening. The heron feeds on fish, frogs, crayfish, and other aquatic life."

I tapped Uncle Steve on the arm and pointed to the heron. "Now I know what happened to the frogs and toads that were supposed to be in the last exhibit."

He smiled and nodded his head.

The voice was back when we moved to the next exhibit. "Because of its nocturnal status, the screech owl relies in large part to its acute hearing. Owls also have a distinctive facial disk, which helps to direct sound towards their ears. By day, screech owls sit quietly among the branches of a tree. If danger threatens, these little owls protect themselves by elongating their bodies and extending their ear tufts to resemble and blend into the tree branches. They shut their eyes down to a mere slit and remain perfectly still until the threat has passed. By night, they are fierce hunters. The screech owl is one of the smallest owls, measuring eight to nine inches in length. The sound of the screech owl is quite spectacular. You may have heard it before. It sounds like this...*SCREECHHHHH!*"

This screech reverberated throughout the room. It was cool. They did it twice.

"We've heard that sound before, when we were on your deck haven't we?" I asked Uncle Steve.

"Yes we have, but not quite as loud," he responded with a pained expression on his face.

We moved on to the next exhibit and that's when we saw the bats. Their habitat looked just like a cave - pretty cool. I pointed. "Look at all of them."

The voice continued. "These big brown bats are hiding in a cave. Bats are our only true flying mammals. They are also one of the most numerous, second only to rodents."

"That's a lot of bats," I observed.

The voice continued. "Big brown bats spend the daylight hours sleeping in dark, secluded areas. They come out just before dark in search of insects. They navigate through the night skies by use of echolocation, a method by which ultrasonic sounds emitted through the mouth or nose of the bat are bounced off objects in the bats' flight path."

I pointed to one part of the cave and said to Uncle Steve, "Hey look. Is that Dracula?"

He looked for just a moment as if I was noticing something special. Then he just gave me that look – that 'nice try' look.

Next was the skunk exhibit. The voice went on. "Meet our striped skunk. When disturbed, the striped skunk will usually stamp its front feet at the intruder as a warning. If the intruder doesn't heed to the warning, **watch out**! The skunk is probably going to spray a foul-smelling musk at its enemies. This musk is secreted from a pair of anal glands under the tail. This musk can be sprayed as far as ten to fifteen feet and the odor can be detected up to a mile away."

Steve said, "He doesn't have to tell us that does he, Austin? You proved that a couple of weeks ago."

The voice continued. "Therefore, if you are ever out walking at night and smell a skunk, it could be a long way away or it could be right behind you. You never know."

We had moved through almost the entire area. Two exhibits were left. The voice was telling us, "Owls are unique birds. To the left of the skunk, you will find a barred owl. Owls are noted for their large head and large eyes, which are fixed in the skull, making it necessary for them to rotate their heads in order to change their view. The barred owl gets its name from the barring or banding of alternating colors over most of the bird's body. They range from sixteen to twenty–five inches in length with a wingspan of thirty-eight to fifty inches."

"Look at that guy," I remarked, pointing to the barred owl. "He's not quite as big as the great horned owl back in Mountview, but he's just as cool."

The last exhibit was the Virginia opossum. The voice was saying something about it being the only marsupial found in the United States, but then I didn't hear anything else. I was still looking at the barred owl. I remembered Becca at the Nature Center in Mountview calling the owl 'Night Tiger.' I wondered if 'Night Tiger' was for all owls.

When I looked around for Uncle Steve to ask him, I noticed him talking with Amy and Mr. Baker. I walked over towards them as the voice finished the show in the background. "We hope you have enjoyed your trip through the world of night. This unique experience allows you to see up close the animals that are not frequently seen by human eyes."

I realized that Katie was still over at the snake exhibit so I continued walking towards the group.

Amy was speaking. "So we will keep her under observation for a day and see if she improves. We will need to leave her here." She saw me approach. "Austin, we gave Sarah some new medicine and we will watch her to see how she responds. Nothing serious, but we'll need to keep her here for the next twelve hours. I'm sure that she'll be fine."

"OK," I said. "Is she sleeping or can I go see her now?"

"Actually, she is resting and we shouldn't disturb her. OK? She'll be fine," Amy assured me.

"I understand." I looked up to find Katie walking toward us.

"Great, we're all here," Amy observed as Katie joined the group. "Mr. Baker and I are going to our meeting but you guys get to stay as long as you want. Mr. Baker has asked one of his staff to take you on a tour of the Center. Greg Murdock will be joining you guys and will meet you here in a few minutes."

Uncle Steve asked, "Where will we meet up with you?"

"I'll meet you at the hotel. We have a guest speaker coming for dinner so I'll be a little late."

"That's fine with us; we'll get a personal guided tour and see you later. Don't worry about us. We'll be just fine," Uncle Steve said. He turned to Mr. Baker. "Ron, you have a great facility here. Thanks for letting us enjoy it." He held out his hand and Mr. Baker shook it.

"The pleasure is mine," Mr. Baker smiled. "Enjoy our Center. See you kids later."

We said our goodbyes. Uncle Steve reached out for Amy's hand. They held hands for a second, then Amy winked at Uncle Steve as she and Mr. Baker departed.

"So, we're on our own," Uncle Steve said, rubbing his hands together. "What should we see first?"

"Let's go see the snakes," Katie suggested

"No way!" I jumped in. "Let's go see the wolves."

A voice behind us said, "Well, personally, I would want to go see the cougar."

We turned around simultaneously to find a friendly, smiling face. "Hi, I'm Greg Murdock, your personal guide for the day."

Katie said, "Yeah, let's see Carrie the Cougar."

"So you and Carrie know each other, do you?" asked Mr. Murdock. "Hello, Steve – I heard you were coming today."

"Greg, it's good to see you. You still taking good care of my girl?" Uncle Steve inquired, referring to Carrie.

"Your girl? Where did you get that idea? Carrie is my girl. Go ask her yourself," Mr. Murdock grinned.

He shook Uncle Steve's hand and you could see that they were friends, probably for a long time. I guess what they were talking about was the family that first raised Carrie. They gave her to Uncle Steve after realizing that she would get so big that they wouldn't be able to take care of her anymore. Uncle Steve couldn't take care of a big cat either, so he gave her to this Nature Center, which makes sense.

Well, anyway, we all left to go see Carrie the Cougar.

Chapter 4

Sarah knew something wasn't right.

She had been feeling bad for several weeks now. Amy had tried to help, but nothing seemed to work. Sarah realized that she was now in a different place. Perhaps Amy had found some people who could help her. The examination was over and Amy and the doctor had left.

Sarah could feel something changing. Her body was moving and developing without her control. She watched as her tail became longer and flatter.

She knew that she was slowly becoming a Schmooney. She had to get this to stop. If someone were to see her…well, she didn't like to think of that.

She suddenly had a craving for licorice!

* * * * *

Once outside, I could see that there were a lot more exhibits out there. "Mr. Murdock, how big is this place?"

"Austin, we have about forty-two acres of wildlife here in Asheville. You just saw our Main Exhibition Building, and, if you want to walk this way, we are headed to the Predator Habitat where we keep the wolves, cougars, and bobcats."

"Predator habitat – cool!" I grinned.

We walked past some picnic tables. "This is the picnic area, for anyone who wants to bring their lunch so they can have a whole day in the wild. Over to the left, up there," Mr. Murdock pointed, "is the river otter pool and behind that is the turtle pond, then next to that is the fox habitat, and then the raccoon habitat."

We were walking past an outside classroom area when Mr. Murdock said, "We have lectures and presentations by our naturalists and guest speakers which we sometimes have outside here to your left. And you can see, over there to our right, the back of the raptor habitat where our eagles, owls, hawks, and vultures live."

Katie gulped. "Vultures?"

"Cool," I said.

Up ahead, about twenty yards away, was a big gate with a sign above it which read 'Predator Habitat.' I thought that it would be cool to have another sign saying, 'Trespassers Will Be Eaten.'

Mr. Murdock pointed to our right. "Over in that area we have the black bear habitat and, to the right of it, we keep the white-tailed deer and the wild turkeys. If you like, we will get to see all of them before you leave."

"I like bears," Katie remarked.

We stopped at a metal gate and Mr. Murdock said, "OK, we are now entering the predator habitat. You don't have to worry about getting too close to the cages; simply stay on the walk. The animals have the cage around them and over them so they are secured. Plus, we also have an electric wire running about two feet inside the cage perimeter. So the animals cannot get close to the cage. That allows fingers that do get inside the bars to stay with the person who brought them."

I knew exactly what he meant. I put my hands together. Yep, still had all ten fingers, so let's keep it that way.

We walked by the bobcat habitat and looked inside. Mr. Murdock was talking about the bobcats, but I didn't hear him. I looked over at the cage next to the bobcats and saw the most amazingly awesome animal stretched out across the ground – it was the cougar!

She was magnificent. Her long tail was wrapped around her body with only the end of it moving ever so slightly, as if she were slowly fanning herself. Her face was like a mask, finely sculpted, covered with golden fur and black markings. Her fur, ever so soft, was gleaming in the early day's sun. She was the queen of her world, and she knew it.

Mr. Murdock apparently saw my interest. He walked over and stood next to me. "She is one beautiful cat, isn't she, Austin?"

"Yes, sir, one beautiful golden gato," I agreed.

"That's Spanish for cat - el gato, the cat," Katie bragged as she walked by.

"Why don't I tell you what I know about Carrie and, if there is anything you want me to explain, just stop me, OK?" Mr. Murdock asked our group. "Carrie came to us when she was a seven-week-old kitten, thanks to your Uncle Steve. She is a hybrid Western and South American cougar. She was thoroughly imprinted on people and still shows many playful, kitten-like behaviors. She is, however, essentially a wild animal with deeply ingrained, predatory instincts. Attempts by people to make pets out of animals like these usually fail and we strongly discourage that practice. The cougar is known by many names, including panther, puma, and catamount, painter, and mountain lion. Although once found throughout much of North America, cougars are now absent from many regions where they once were common, including Western North Carolina."

Carrie got up and walked over to where we were standing, as if she knew we wanted to get a closer look at her, which we did.

Mr. Murdock continued. "As you can see, Carrie is a large, muscular cat. Cougars average seven to nine feet in total length of which up to a third is tail and they weigh between one hundred and fifty to two hundred pounds when full grown. Carrie is tan colored with black coloration on the sides of her muzzle, the backs of her ears, and the tip of her tail. Cougars are secretive, solitary hunters that feed primarily on white-tailed deer, but will also eat smaller game such as opossums, rabbits, mice, and even insects if food supplies are limited. Cougars are skilled night hunters with excellent eyesight and superb hearing. They run swiftly, are agile climbers, and can even swim. Rather than simply chasing after their food, cougars prefer stalking their prey at close range, utilizing the element of surprise. At the last moment, a cougar may leap as far as twenty feet or more onto the animal's back. Strong jaws and long canine teeth then make it possible for cougars to kill their prey with one bite to the nape of the neck. After an initial feeding, a cougar may cover the carcass with leaves or other debris to be saved for a later meal. Since white-tailed deer, a primary food source for the cougar, have made a dramatic comeback, perhaps the cougar will soon follow."

Carrie lay down next to a rock and I heard a deep, contented sound coming from inside her throat. "Mr. Murdock, is she purring?"

He paused to listen, then nodded. "Yes, she is purring."

Then, as if on cue, Carrie got up, looked at us, and meowed. I am not kidding - she meowed in the same voice as Franklin, my cat. We laughed. She meowed again. It was a high-pitched, girlish meow. It didn't sound threatening at all.

"Don't let that meow fool you. Although Carrie is very friendly and imprinted which makes her look and act domesticated, cougars are dangerous animals. That meow sounds so innocent, but cougars can be deadly," Mr. Murdock warned.

"In this part of the country, the cougars and the gray wolves would have been the most aggressive predators. However, the Eastern cougar disappeared from here around the turn of the century. Even so, we are always hearing about cougar sightings. The common thought is that this true Eastern cougar, which was a separate geographical subspecies, could still be here in a small population and now making a comeback due to the increased deer population which is its primary food source. Or are these sightings actually a Western cougar, which was released after being someone's pet?

"People get these animals and keep them as pets, which is against the law. These animals become big and people will release them into the wild. There have been sighting of cougars with kittens crossing the parkway near Mt. Pisgah. The bottom line is that no one can prove if they are here or not. There are some wildlife officials or trained wildlife biologists who are credible who have had sightings, but not until one is captured or killed, by a hunter, or hit by an automobile, will we know. It will remain a mystery. My opinion is there are cougars up in those mountains." And he pointed to the mountains behind us.

Mr. Murdock paused. All of us just looked at Carrie. She turned around and slowly walked away. *Golden Gato*, I thought.

"OK, does anyone want to see the wolves?" Mr. Murdock asked.

We walked to the next habitat - the gray wolves habitat. This was another big area surrounded by a fence. The area was so big I couldn't see the other end of the cage. The habitat was carved out of the side of a hill. There were enormous rocks, a small waterfall, trees, and grasses. It looked like a big natural area.

Mr. Murdock pointed to a large wolf. "The big, gray wolf, who happens to be walking over to us, his name is Caruso. He is the alpha male, which means he is in charge. His pack has two females which you can see are right over there." He pointed to them, about twenty yards away.

"You can see that Caruso is a large, broad-headed animal that displays much variation in coat color, from gray to brownish gray and brownish white to grayish white. They hold their tails carried high when running, and have front feet that are larger than their hind feet. Most males are between seventy and one hundred and twenty-five pounds, with females being noticeably smaller. He weighs in at the high end of the scale."

The other two wolves, the females, began to approach us. They were definitely smaller. Caruso was standing right in front of us with his front paws on a rock, as if he was showing off.

Mr. Murdock continued. "Wolves live and hunt in groups call packs. Wolf packs usually have specific territories ranging in size from fifty to one thousand square miles. Gray wolves rely on three types of communication: verbal, scent marking, and body postures."

"Excuse me, Mr. Murdock," I interrupted. "But what is Caruso saying with his body posture now?"

Caruso was still standing on the rock right in front of us. He didn't seem to be afraid of us. He probably wasn't afraid of anything.

"Austin, he might be saying, 'This is my turf - I am in charge.' Caruso slowly turned his head and looked at me. "Now he's saying, 'I am hungry - do you have any little boys for me?'" Mr. Murdock said jokingly.

I smiled. "Nice try."

Mr. Murdock turned to Caruso and told us, "A gray wolf can attain speeds of forty-five miles per hour in short distance sprints. Lone, dispersing wolves have traveled five hundred miles to find a mate and new territory. That sharp tooth that comes to a point, found on the front of the upper and lower jaw, is used for tearing meat. Those two teeth, one on each side of his mouth, are called carnassials and are almost two and one half inches long. The jaws can exert an estimated one thousand, five hundred pounds of pressure per inch. And, before you get too worried, let me tell you that a healthy wolf attacking a human has never been documented." He paused to let us think about that for a moment.

"Of course not. How could a victim document an attack if the victim is eaten?" Uncle Steve joked.

I groaned, then turned to Caruso again. Boy, he was big! "Mr. Murdock, gray wolves have been extirpated haven't they?"

"Wow, that's a big word," he commented. Without pausing he continued. "Yes, they were last seen in this area about one hundred years ago, when they were hunted to extinction, here in the Carolinas. But wolves are able to survive in a large variety of habitats and climate extremes - second only to humans. So they aren't extinct; they live in other parts of the world."

He paused and pointed to Caruso's toes. "Hairs between their toes are for below-freezing temperatures." He looked up. "Before blood reaches the outer layers of tissue in the foot, it is pre-cooled, lessening the difference in temperature inside and out, and reducing the risk of freezing. Wolves are the only members of the dog family with this adaptation."

Dog family, I thought. *So Edison is related to a big gray wolf. I better not tell him that - it would go straight to his head.*

I asked, "How smart are these wolves? I have found out that crows are very smart, which surprised me. How about Caruso, here? Can he figure things out?"

"Oh yes, wolves are very clever. Caruso, especially, is very intelligent. Let me give you an example. I remember one day, we were feeding the wolves large cow femur bones." Mr. Murdock spread his arms apart and showed us with his hands how big the bones were. "They look like dinosaur bones. Well, as you can see," he pointed to one side of the habitat, "this side of their habitat has got a big slope to it and the bone rolled down the hill as they were all tugging on it. The bone rolled and ended up on the other side of this hot wire." He was pointing to a wire that was raised above the ground that ran around the entire perimeter. He had mentioned it before when we were in the cougar habitat. "The reason we have the wires here is that they are used to keep the wolves away from the fence. People are on the other side of the fence and sometimes will put their fingers through the fence. The wolves would bite their fingers off. Then our attendance would drop off, people wouldn't come, and I would be out of a job."

I smiled. I liked his sense of humor.

Mr. Murdock continued his story, "So, the wolves went bounding down the hill after the bone that was continuing to roll. Well, the bone went past the electrical wire so they all put their brakes on to stop, because they knew that the electrical wire would zing them and they don't like that. The wolves couldn't get to the bone. We were watching as they were trying to figure out how to get the bone. They were walking back and forth, sizing up the situation. They were digging at it, bouncing around in front of the bone, wondering how they could get to it. So the alpha male here, Caruso, analyzed the situation, then grabbed a long stick in his mouth and went over to the closest point to the bone and started hitting it and tapping it." Mr. Murdock was demonstrating with his hands. "Eventually, he tapped the bone back till it cleared the fence. Very impressive skill set."

He paused as we let that sink in, marveling at Caruso as he allowed us to admire him. "It is not just chimpanzees that are so intelligent - it's the wolves, it's the crows, and the owls, too. That is another interesting part of my job. We just never quit learning. I am always amazed at what animals do know and feel and how they express those feelings. I am a skeptic and reserved as to comparing animals to humans. But I am always amazed at how they are so aware and how they are so in touch with each other. There is another form of communication out there. It might be telepathy, it might be ESP, I don't know what it is, but another sense is working in the animal world."

Caruso opened his mouth and yawned as if he had heard it all before. Katie pointed and said, "Oh, look at his teeth!"

Mr. Murdock watched Caruso's wide-open mouth slowly close and said, "Wolves have forty-two teeth of four different types, designed to tear, puncture, shear, and crush. They have no teeth designed for chewing, so chunks of meat are swallowed whole."

"Wow, they eat like Austin does!" Katie laughed and so did the others.

I didn't think it was that funny.

At the habitat, to the left of where we were standing, there was a large exhibit sign and at the base was a button. It said PUSH, so I did.

It was a recording of several wolves howling. The sound was scary and I felt the hairs stand up on the back of my neck. It was a high-pitched, eerie sound. I have heard dogs howl before and this was similar, except it seemed to be much, much more fatal.

"Mr. Murdock, it's obvious you know a lot about these animals. So what exactly is your job?" I wondered.

"Austin, I am the Education Curator, Volunteer Coordinator, Summer Camp Coordinator, Senior Naturalist, and I even get to clean out cages."

"I know the feeling – at least the clean out the cages part," I informed him.

He smiled. "Now, if you want, we can go back and see any of the habitats that we passed on the way in here. Do I hear any requests?"

"I want to see the bears," Katie insisted. So we headed off towards the bears.

* * * * *

Woodrow and Calvin Garner weren't the 'sharpest knives in the drawer,' as the old saying goes. Matter of fact, their momma tried her best to keep her two boys away from anything sharp. She figured that they would only hurt themselves. Or worse, they would go hurt someone else.

When they were younger, the term, 'not smart enough to come in out of the rain,' came to mind whenever anyone set their sights on them. Momma Garner had tried to raise two fine boys in the image of their father, but due to his multiple arrests, she was left with the responsibility of having to raise, feed, clothe, and keep the two boys alive and out of jail - all by herself.

When you are alone and have to do all of those things all by yourself, well, something might not get the attention it needs. And, in this case, it was Woodrow and Calvin's education. Momma Garner tried to raise her boys proper for many years. Finally, she just gave up.

As the boys got older, their good traits seemed to get sidetracked and their bad traits seemed to take over.

Woodrow was the older of the Garner boys. As Woodrow got older, he changed only physically. He was always taller and stronger than his younger brother. But the boy just never developed mentally. He was much slower than his brother. He was also lazy and just downright mean.

Being slow isn't a bad thing. Woodrow still could have made something out of his life. He could have developed into someone that his momma would have been proud of.

But he chose not to.

Now Calvin, on the other hand, had his daddy's striking good looks. His momma said that Calvin could have been anything he wanted to be, because he also had his daddy's knack for figuring things out and getting what he wanted. Calvin was very smart. Calvin was also very charming.

Unfortunately, he didn't have the discipline to do anything useful. He could have held a real job. He could have found himself a wife, settled down, and raised a fine family. He could have moved out of their little mountain town and started somewhere new – in a bigger city – somewhere with a future.

If he had chosen to stay in town, he could have been a fishing or hunting guide. He was raised in upper Cherokee County and knew the woods like the back of his hand. He had fished Lake Toxaway, Lake Minti, Natahala Lake, and, even Lake Jocassee. He knew them all.

Calvin could have been a lot of things. But the problem was, he just wasn't interested.

He inherited many good things from his daddy. But he also inherited a lot of bad things from his daddy. He inherited his daddy's lack of morals. He inherited his daddy's mean streak. He inherited his daddy's selfishness - never caring for anyone else but himself.

But with all those bad things, he also inherited his daddy's desire to be somebody. And before his daddy was arrested the third time for 'revenuing' and taken to jail, his daddy *was* somebody. It wasn't legal, but, according to momma, his daddy was somebody.

He also inherited his daddy's desire to cheat, steal, lie, and not worry about the consequences. He loved to cheat. And his brother was dumb enough to cheat with him, which was very convenient for Calvin. Because, with Woodrow around, he always had someone to blame when things didn't go the way he wanted.

It was perfect. No reason to change. Life was good.

But life could always be better. And Calvin had an idea just how to make that happen.

Chapter 5

Greg Murdock looked at his watch. He realized that he had completely forgotten about the time due to all the fun he was having, and several things needed to be done before the Center closed. He used his two-way radio to contact Leonard Hunt. Leonard was in a meeting with Jimmy Lucas but they both said that they would come see us and finish the tour for him. Mr. Murdock excused himself from the group and asked us to stay at the white-tailed deer habitat where two other staff members would meet us and finish the tour. That was fine. Mr. Murdock was a great host and we had a lot of fun with him.

We were standing on the elevated wooden boardwalk above the deer habitat. This gave us a great view of the deer walking around their habitat, since we were standing about fifteen feet above them. I was standing next to the railing and, from here I could see the wild turkeys in the next habitat. I have seen those birds before. They are all around Mountview. I heard footsteps on the boardwalk and turned to see two men approaching.

Mr. Hunt and Mr. Lucas introduced themselves to us. They asked us what we had seen so far and if we had any questions. I had one.

"Have you ever had an animal get loose? When you were feeding them or maybe when you transported them or cleaned the cage, did they ever get out? How do you catch them then?" I wondered.

Mr. Lucas spoke matter-of-factly, smiling reassuringly. "Well, we usually catch them. We almost never lose one permanently, none that I can remember. We usually recover them without harm to the animal or to the population. Now, with electric fences, and backup doors and locks, and better capture equipment, we almost never have an animal escape. But it does happen every once in awhile at any facility like this one."

Mr. Hunt added, "The deer got out once, the door wasn't secured, but they all came back." He paused for a moment and then continued, "That sounds kind of funny doesn't it? Well, it makes sense when you think about it. Because, to the deer, this is where the food is." Mr. Hunt pointed to their habitat. "This has been their home. And this is **their** territory. If you let them out, they just don't know what to do or where to go, so they come back here, to their home."

"Let me give you another example. The black bear," Mr. Lucas began, pointing to the bear habitat at the end of the boardwalk. "Well, he got out once and just went out for a leisurely walk. You can imagine what we were thinking - the bear is out! But no one panicked. We found him casually walking down one of our paths, like that one over there. We knew he was out, but this place is big. We had been looking for him and we were walking in the opposite direction coming down the same path he was on - we were headed right for him and didn't know it. When we walked up a slight hill, we came face to face with the bear! Wow! That was a surprise. We didn't know what to do so we just stared at the bear and he just stared back at us. None of us, including the bear, knew what to do next. So we just started yelling and waving our arms. Fortunately for us, the bear became frightened and he turned and started running back to his pen. He ran not only to his pen, but he continued to run all the way into his den, and, if he could have, I bet he would have slammed the door behind him!" We laughed. "Animals are typically not aggressive unless they have something to protect. It is just not in their nature to protect something that is not theirs. They aren't comfortable in new surroundings so they come back to where they are comfortable."

Mr. Hunt jumped in. "Now it is totally different with the rehab animals. A rehab animal is a wild animal that has been injured or orphaned and found. We successfully raise these animals or nurse the injured to the point of being able to fend for themselves in the natural world. This is one of our most rewarding and useful experiences. We keep them only as long as necessary, so that they can go back to the wild, where they belong. We keep them in a separate area also, away from human contact to avoid imprinting." Mr. Hunt paused, noticing the expression on my face. "Something you want to ask me?"

"Imprinting – I've heard the word, but I forgot what it means," I replied.

"Sure. In wild animals this process is one by which the young animal identifies with the adult of its own species. They will learn by imitation and observation the methods for finding food, shelter, safety, and means of survival including mating and defensive behaviors. If care is not taken, the process of imprinting can be transferred to the human who raises and releases young animals. Animals that do not imprint on their own species will lack survival skills. In other words, they will die in the wild," Mr. Hunt explained.

"So, how do you prevent that from happening?" I wondered.

"We raise all animals with at least one other member of the same species. Animals placed together should be about the same age. We handle all rehab animals as little as possible. When it comes to feeding, some rehabilitators wear a 'ghost' costume with camouflage material. The person is completely covered except for eyeholes and arm slits. Those types of things."

"What's the biggest bear that you have ever seen?" Katie inquired.

Mr. Lucas pointed over to the bear habitat. "Well, our bear weighs about as much as any I have ever seen, and he is around six hundred pounds."

Mr. Hunt added, "Someone did kill a bear near Gatlinburg at about the same weight. So six hundred pounds is common. Now, it was illegal for that man to kill a bear, and he was later arrested. Even though the animal was coming into inhabited areas, the bear was not in-season; bears are a protected species. There is a legal bear season, although it is only two days. By the way, eight hundred pounds seems to be the largest that I have ever heard of."

"Why do people kill bears? Is it for their meat?" I asked.

"Actually, they hunt the black bear largely for its bladder which is used for medicinal purposes in the Far East. There seems to be a market for about everything these days," Mr. Hunt replied.

Uncle Steve wanted to change the subject from killing bears. "What are some of the stories that you hear? Stories that might be legends from the people that live around here."

Both men thought about that question for a moment. Then Mr. Lucas said, "One that comes to mind immediately is one from an older lady - she was about eighty years old. She lived over near Crowder, used to tell the story of growing up in the old days. Her family used to have to keep a pot of boiling water on the fireplace so that the wolves wouldn't climb down the chimney and eat them. Now, this lady was serious, mind you. I know that seems to sound just like a children's fable or a nursery rhyme, and I think she was just confused. But who knows? She may have tied a true story to the fable. It happens that way with legends."

Mr Hunt added, "We do hear stories, none come to mind right now, but we also get lots of phone calls from people that just don't know how to deal with the animals. For example, I got a call from a lady that had a raccoon in a tree in their backyard. She was worried about its safety. I might add that we are always pleased to get calls from people wanting to protect the animals. Well, it seems that her husband was also concerned about the raccoon, because it wouldn't come down out of one of their trees. The raccoon had been up there going on three days. The husband was so upset that he got his ladder and put food and water up on a nearby limb. The lady wanted to know why it wasn't coming down. Tell you the truth, I had no idea, so I just starting asking questions. I was talking to the lady, kept asking her questions, and come to find out that she kept her German Shepherd dog leashed to the very same tree that the raccoon was in!" He shook his head. "People want to do what is right. They just don't think everything through. So, as long as people keep moving into the animals' habitats, we will continue to get phone calls from people asking for help. They just don't know."

Mr. Lucas nodded. "One of my favorite stories, and I have heard it several time, is that people think there is actually a real hoop snake. It seems that a hoop snake is a snake that can connect its head to its tail, which makes this big hoop and then the snake can roll down a hill like a hoop."

We laughed.

Katie arched her arms above her head, then she touched her fingers together. I guess she was trying to see what a hoop would look like.

Uncle Steve remarked, "Austin is very interested in owls - do you have any owl stories?"

Mr. Hunt looked at Mr. Lucas and asked, "You've been taloned, haven't you, Jimmy?"

Mr. Lucas shook his head in agreement. "I was working with the Little General, our great horned owl, one day. We groom their beaks and talons, and vaccinate our animals for West Nile Virus. Well, when the General got on my arm, he got on higher than usual. The leather glove that I wear to protect my arm from his razor sharp talons wasn't that high up here." He showed us his arm, indicating that one of the owl's feet must have gripped his arm above his elbow. "Well, one of his talons went into my arm. There is no way you can get a talon out; the owl is just too powerful. You know, it takes two of us just to pull the talons back once they are hooked on a net."

"So, what happened?" I asked.

"Well, there was nothing for me to do. So I offered the owl some food, dangling it just out of his reach. He had to move down my arm, towards my hand, to get it. When he moved, he released his hold on me."

Mr. Hunt added, "I believe that Eddie got taloned too. He wasn't as fortunate. Eddie still has the scar where the talon went through his arm."

"There is a reason that they call them Night Tigers," Uncle Steve added.

"So, where would you like to go from here?" Mr. Lucas asked.

"Let's see, we haven't seen the otters or the foxes or the turtle pond. Let's head over in that direction," Uncle Steve suggested.

As we walked, Mr. Lucas said, "The turtle pond reminds me of a story. We get a lot of schools here. Field trips are common and it is something that Leonard promotes heavily. It is great community service and we all learn a lot from the experience. Well, one day, a teacher had brought her students to the Center. It was a good group - they were asking some really good questions." We were approaching the turtle pond. "When they got here," Mr. Lucas pointed to one end of the pond, "Leonard was explaining about the turtles, the tadpoles, and the frogs. He was explaining about the animal life here in this pond. Well, the teacher wanted to show his knowledge, so he told his class, 'Look at all the tadpoles; one day they will all grow up to be real big turtles!"

He paused while we all laughed, except for Katie who wasn't laughing. She was still just looking into the pond.

Mr. Hunt noticed that and said, "As you know, Katie, tadpoles don't become turtles - they become frogs."

Katie smiled and seemed relieved.

Mr. Hunt continued. "So, like I said, we all learn a lot from people visiting the Nature Center."

As we watched the otters play in their habitat, my thoughts drifted back to Sarah. I wondered how she was doing.

Perhaps Uncle Steve noticed that I was looking off in the distance. He said, "Jimmy, Leonard, we've had a lot of fun and have learned a lot. I will recommend to everyone I meet to take the time to come to the Western North Carolina Nature Center here in Asheville. So much goes on around us - it would benefit everyone to know more about the natural world."

"Thank you for saying that, Steve," Mr. Lucas said appreciatively. "We, of course, agree with you. The last time I looked, this is the only planet that we have to live on, so we better make the best of it. Our facility helps promote preservation through education. We want people to learn. We want people to respect what nature has given us. We will do our best to accomplish that task, here at the Center."

We finished the day right there at the river otter habitat. We thanked Mr. Lucas and Mr. Hunt and went back to the Main Exhibition Hall.

* * * * *

Sarah was getting dizzy. *Where is that licorice smell coming from?* she wondered.

The cage was starting to spin. Sarah felt hotter than usual, and she needed a drink of water. As she stood to move towards the water, her legs began to buckle. Bracing herself with her front paw, she held tightly onto the wire sides of the cage.

She was able to stand, but then she bumped her head into the top of the cage. She wondered why. That had never happened before. With her other paw, she reached up to rub the area of her head that she had bumped. She didn't expect to feel what she felt.

Oh no!

Her ears were changing, too!

Chapter 6

We went back into the Main Hall where Katie wanted to show Uncle Steve that she could hold the snakes. Apparently, she had 'graduated' to large snakes now and was eager to show Uncle Steve how she could hold one. I didn't want anything to do with the snakes. I wanted to see Sarah and I needed to see her alone. So I asked Uncle Steve if he would mind if I went downstairs. I could see that Uncle Steve wanted to do something other than go to the snake exhibit, too, but he didn't want Katie to feel bad. So, he said it was fine with him, as long as I came directly back as soon as I saw Sarah.

I ran down the stairs, taking two steps at a time, and jumped the last three steps. I looked around and didn't see anyone, so I confidently walked through the door that said 'Observation Room,' expecting to see Sarah in her cage.

Immediately, I noticed her cage door was wide open, her blanket was on the floor, and she was gone!

I looked around the room. I looked on the floor. I looked for any sign that Amy might have taken her for an examination. I even looked in the cabinets and under each table.

No Sarah!

Then I heard it.

CRASH!

The sound came from the adjoining room. I opened the door slowly and saw the back of a skunk, sitting in the middle of the room, busy doing something. The skunk was surrounded by clumps of black dirt and pieces of a broken pot, scattered all over the floor. I knew it was Sarah. She had her back to me, or it might have been her side, I couldn't really tell. But what I could see was that she was eating something. What was she eating?

I looked around and was relieved to see that no one else was in the room. I looked into the other room and didn't see or hear anyone coming. I entered the room and softly closed the door behind me.

This room was filled with small potted plants. They were on tables, hanging from hooks on the wall, and on shelves. There were also books lining the shelves behind me. The plants had colored sticks with colored cards on them. I guess that they contained some information that told what kind of plants they were. Most of the cards and sticks were yellow, but there were a few that were red. The red ones seemed to be on the one table back in the corner. Sarah was on the floor next to that table. A red card and stick were next to her on the floor. They must have fallen to the side when the pot broke.

Sarah hadn't moved since I entered the room. She was still sitting there; I guessed she was eating the leaves of the plant. *'What are you doing?'* I sent.

She turned around to look at me, with portions of partially eaten golden leaves hanging out of her mouth, covering most of her face. Her cheeks were puffed out, full of food. She paused for a moment to stare at me. And then, still looking at me, her little mouth started moving like a sped-up movie. Her jaw was furiously chomping up and down and the fur on her little face was moving right along with it. It was almost funny. But I knew we would both be in trouble if we stayed here.

'We need to get out of here. Somebody had to have heard that crash,' I sent as I walked towards her.

'Just a minute, I need to eat all of this,' she sent back as she continued to devour the plant leaves and stalk.

'Here, I'll help you,' I sent. I was close enough to extend my hand to pick up the remaining pieces of the plant.

Sarah growled!

I mean it. She growled.

I jerked my hand back as quickly as I could. I didn't even know skunks could growl.

'Hey, what's the big idea?' I sent.

'You can't touch this plant. It's poisonous to you. You will get sick.' Sarah paused for a moment to eat the last leaf and she looked at up me. *'Sorry about the growl.'*

'No problem,' I sent, rubbing the hand that had almost gotten bitten. *'So, how can you eat a poisonous plant but I can't touch it?'* " Hey, look at your ears!" I think I said that out loud. Sarah's ears had changed from little, black furry skunk ears to floppy, white and pink rabbit ears. In all the commotion, I hadn't noticed. "What's happening to your ears?"

'No time to explain,' she sent, *'somebody is coming.'*

We both looked at the door and could hear footsteps that were quickly getting louder.

We looked frantically around the room to find someplace to hide and saw....nothing.

No place to hide!

We were stuck.

Sarah, who had eaten all the plant leaves and part of the stalk, was next to me, I sent, *'Jump!'* and held out my arms.

She leapt into my arms and we darted to the only place in the room where we might have a chance to remain unnoticed - next to the wall, right behind the door that was about to open. I hoped that when the door opened we could remain hidden behind it.

It was our only chance!

The footsteps continued to approach. My back was against the wall as I clutched Sarah in my arms. The footsteps stopped and then the doorknob rattled just before the door opened. We stood there in silence, afraid to make a sound, watching the door swing all the way open and stop right in front of our faces. Whoever came into the room decided not to close it. We were lucky.

If we get caught, how am I going to explain those ears? I couldn't stop thinking, as I stared at the pink and white masses that were right in front of my face. Then I looked down at Sarah's tail. It was a beaver tail, all right - just what I suspected. *How am I going to explain her tail?*

All these questions were running through my mind. Questions that I knew I would be asked if we got caught. How could I answer them? I could hear the questions now: Why was I here? What was the skunk doing outside the cage? That's not a skunk...so, what is it? Which one of us had broken the pot? Which one of us ate the leaves? Which one of us was going to die? The questions would never stop. So I did the only thing a kid could do. I closed my eyes and hoped for the best.

We heard the footsteps approach the middle of the room. Then there was silence. Curiosity overcame us. I opened my eyes. Sarah and I both slowly peered around the open door that was providing us this great hiding place, to see what was going on. We could see the back of a lady wearing a white blouse and khaki pants, standing in the middle of the room, right at the edge of the dirt pile. She had stopped to see what was wrong. Her hands were on her hips. She realized that the sound had come from this room and she was scanning the room to see if anything else was broken or out of place. She obviously noticed the broken pot since the black dirt and clay-colored pot pieces were scattered all over the shiny, white tile floor right in front of her. She continued to survey the room - maybe she was looking to see if she could find out why it hit the floor.

She was still glancing around the room when she started walking to her left. She was about to look in our direction. We popped back behind the safety of the open door.

"Oh, no!" she exclaimed.

'Uh oh, she sees us,' I sent.

I knew it; I could hear her approaching our hiding place. The footsteps got louder and louder, and then….

She stopped just short of the other side of the door.

'Here it comes! She's going to close the door and our hiding spot will be revealed, I just know it!' I wasn't sure if I was just thinking or sending this message.

'Relax. We're OK. Stay calm,' Sarah reassured me.

The footsteps were now moving back to the center of the room – away from us. We heard something bang on the floor. It sounded like a metal trashcan. We wanted to look around the door but were afraid she would look in our direction. We looked anyway.

This time, the woman was in the middle of the room, kneeling down, picking up pieces of the pot when we heard, 'BANG!' She dropped one piece into the metal trashcan. 'BANG!' Another piece. 'BONG!' A bigger piece.

She began talking aloud. "No one is allowed in this room." That was followed with, "Why do I have to be…." She paused and we watched her stop to look at something that had caught her attention.

She was looking at the wooden chair that was closest to her, about ten feet away. She reached under the chair and retrieved the bright red card and red stick. Apparently, that meant something. She immediately pulled her hands back but she kept staring at the card.

"Oh, no!" she cried out. She jumped up and raced towards a sink next to the tables. Her back was to us as she thoroughly washed her hands. She was shaking her head back and forth as if she needed help comprehending the situation. After quickly drying her hands, she reached for the two-way radio that was on her belt.

"Leonard? Leonard?" she repeated. She waited, but there was no sound. "Ron, are you there?" She waited to hear some response.

"Can anyone tell me where Leonard is?" she yelled.

A voice finally responded. "He's feeding the raptors."

The woman didn't say anything else, except for uttering a frustrated groan.

A voice came back on the two-way. "Marcie, can I do something for you?"

"Yes, you can. Who is this?" she demanded.

"This is Roger. I'm over in Leonard's office."

"OK, Roger, I'm in the BioLab. Meet me…no, wait a minute." She thought for a moment. "Our goldenseal plant was dropped or fell or something, and it's now all over the floor. But, what is very interesting is that the leaves and the berries and the stalk – everything is all gone!"

"Gone? What do you mean gone?" questioned the voice.

"Gone…vanished…disappeared. That's what I mean. Something either took them or ate them. But they are definitely gone," she said.

"Well, if someone ate them, they're going to be pretty sick very soon. So it won't be hard to find out who it was." There was a pause. "If you have touched it, make sure you wash your hands. I'll give you some help. I'm on my way to your office now."

"Roger," she said, returning her radio to her belt. She then said to no one but herself, "Or maybe I should have said, 'Roger, Roger.'"

She took a quick look around the room as we ducked back behind the door. She then walked out of the room, closing the door behind her. We were both left standing there…drained…relieved. Well, I was left standing there and Sarah was left being held there. Whatever…this was our time to make our break.

Maintaining my hold on Sarah, I slowly opened the door and peered into the Observation Room. No one was there. I saw the open cage and knew what needed to be done. I eased out of the room and softly closed the door behind me. I placed Sarah in her cage as quietly as possible, then I closed the cage door. I was so focused on not making any noise that I didn't hear the approaching footsteps until they were right behind me.

I was standing next to Sarah's cage with my back to whoever was walking into the room. Sarah lay down and still looked real sick. I noticed her ears; they were rabbit ears, all right. *I can't let anyone see her like this*, I thought.

I could hear the person behind me stop before they went into the BioLab Room. I felt them looking at me and knew that they probably wondered where I came from. My heart was beating real fast. I just kept starring at Sarah and didn't turn around or look up. Sarah sent, *'Relax, Austin. They can't see me now. You are fine. Just do what a kid would do. Keep calm.'*

"Excuse me," the same female voice from earlier began, which apparently belonged to Marcie. "How long have *you* been here?"

My back was to her. I slowly turned around. "Oh, hi," I said in my most innocent voice.

"Hi. How long have you been here and what are you doing, if you don't mind me asking?" Marcie asked.

"Not long," I replied. Then I decided to get creative. "I saw you walk in the door and I waved, but I guess you didn't see me. And then you ran out and I waved again." I was shaking my head back and forth. That was always a convincing touch. "Is everything OK?" I added. I had plenty of practice here.

"I didn't see you here before," she said, motioning with her finger as if to indicate when she entered the room and left it.

"Well, I have to be real quiet, because of my sick pet skunk here." I pointed to the cage. Sarah was under her blanket and those ears and her tail were out of sight. "I'm here with Amy Bryant. You left in a big hurry; you probably just didn't see me standing here. Is everything OK?" I repeated.

She stopped looking at me and peered at the closed door of the BioLab room. The other person with her, a guy somewhere around college age, who was probably Roger, walked to the BioLab door, opened it, and entered to investigate further. Marcie kept her eyes on me as she slowly walked towards me. "Did anyone go in or out of that room? Have you seen anyone come through that door?"

"Except you, no, ma'am, but I did hear something break and it sounded like it came from in there, " I said convincingly.

"Yes, yes, did anyone or anything come out of that room?" Marcie asked pointing to the plant room.

"No, ma'am, I'm just taking care of my sick animal here. I didn't see anyone. Sorry."

Marcie seemed to be fine with that. "OK, thanks." Then she turned and walked towards the door. She looked back at me, paused, then she left the room, closing the door behind her.

Whew, I thought and sent, *'That was close.'* I looked into the cage at Sarah who had a gleam in her eye. She winked at me. I winked back. Now that the immediate danger was over, I looked at her ears. *'What's happening to your ears now?'*

She sent, *'What do you mean?'*

'Your ears are now turning back into skunk ears.' I pulled the cover from her tail. *'And your tail is back to normal. What happened?'*

Sarah reached up with her paws and bent her head to feel her ears. *'I was afraid this was going to happen. My body is so weak; I was changing back to my original Schmooney self. The tail was the first to change and then my ears changed. But I when I smelled the plant in that room, I knew it would help me, that it could give me energy. It has worked before. Once I get stronger, I can control my body and it won't change.'*

'Why didn't you tell me that something like this could happen?' I asked.

'There is so much for you to know. I couldn't cover everything with you. Now I just need to rest. Austin, I'm fine now. Thanks for helping me. You are my best friend. Don't worry,' Sarah assured me.

'Don't worry, oh sure. That's easy for you to say,' I sent.

'Austin, listen to me. I'll be fine. Just let me rest. Thanks for everything that you did.' Sarah paused for a moment and added, *'That was a close one.'*

'Yeah, it was.' I looked at the closed door of the BioLab. *She knows best,* I thought. *I'll leave and think about something else. She'll be fine, I'm sure. And if not, what can I do about it anyway?*

I decided it was time to leave.

'Take care of yourself,' I sent.

'Will do,' Sarah replied.

I left quietly.

Chapter 7

The first time that Calvin heard of the Golden Gato was when his daddy was still around. That was about four years ago.

He wasn't too sure what a gato was, but as long as it was made out of gold, it definitely interested him.

When he first heard about it, he was with his daddy in one of the local bars. Calvin wasn't old enough to be in the bar, but since his daddy did so much business there – selling illegal whiskey - he was permitted to hang around.

A seemingly normal trip to the bathroom caused Calvin's daddy to walk past a particular table at the exact moment that a key word was spoken by one of the table's occupants. That key word was 'gold.'

It was sheer luck! Or, as Calvin's daddy would recall, 'it was fate.'

Actually, what it was, was just a casual conversation between two old-timers who were swapping stories at the local bar where they had stopped for a nightcap. Daddy got real excited when he overhead their conversation and completely forgot about the urgency of his trip to the bathroom.

"Howdy, old-timers, how are you doing?" Daddy asked.

One of them said 'howdy' in return.

"Everybody calls me 'Daddy.' I happen to supply this ole bar with liquor. I see that you're drinking some of it right now. How is it?" asked Daddy, oozing charm.

"It's all right," replied the more talkative old-timer. The other one just kept looking at Daddy without saying a word.

"Well, I appreciate you drinking my liquor and, to demonstrate my appreciation, how about I bring another round over here, on-the-house?" Daddy asked enthusiastically.

They looked at each other and the same man as before replied, "That'll be all right."

That was what Daddy had been waiting for. So he sent Calvin to the bar to fetch another round.

"Mind if I sit a spell?" he inquired, pulling up a chair and sitting before they could respond.

"As I said, they call me Daddy. And, who am I addressing, if you please?" He directed his question to the more talkative man while extending his hand.

"Lester is my name," the man replied, shaking Daddy's hand.

Daddy looked over to the other old-timer. "And, who is this fine gentleman?"

"That's Henry. He don't talk much," Lester added unnecessarily.

And with that, the fateful relationship was born.

Daddy kept supplying the old-timers with whiskey in hopes that they would supply him with more information about the gold mine.

Now, while Daddy was happy with his initial success, it became clear to Lester and Henry that the more they talked, the more liquor this fine gentleman was willing to give them. So, Lester starting telling stories and, after awhile, even Henry joined in. The two old-timers just couldn't believe their luck. They were quite happy to keep talking as long as the whiskey kept pouring. So they talked and they talked and they talked. And Daddy kept sending Calvin to the bar to get more whiskey and more whiskey and more whiskey.

The problem for Daddy was not that the old-timers kept talking; it was the topic of their conversations that frustrated him. He would ask them questions about the gold mine, careful not to be too obvious, but the old-timers would only give a brief answer and then move the conversation in another direction.

"…so we told the man with the horse that he would never take another trip to Prospect again," said Lester, wrapping up one of his lengthy stories.

"So, that was Prospect, huh? Did I hear that there was a gold mine near Prospect?" asked Daddy, trying to return the conversation back to gold.

"You know, I can't blame that man for not wanting to take a trip to Prospect," Henry remarked.

"Didn't I hear that there was a gold mine near Prospect?" Daddy repeated, again trying to shift the conversation to the subject of gold.

"Prospect, North Carolina? Why, I liked Prospect, but I would rather be back in Mountview," Lester said.

"Did I hear you say gold?" Daddy boldly interjected.

"I know what you mean. None of us liked Prospect back then. You know, that reminds me of a story…" and then Henry began to tell another tale.

It went on like this for hours. Daddy wasn't getting anywhere. No matter how charming he was, and no matter how much whiskey he poured these fellows, they just kept dodging the questions about the gold mine. And, before Daddy knew it, the bar was closing and the old-timers went home.

So Daddy did the only thing that he could do. He changed tactics. He decided to become their best friend. He was going to win their trust by getting to know these old-timers. Daddy had the time, that wasn't the problem. He could keep his illegal liquor business going and still make trips to the old-timers' home. He wasn't going to get outsmarted by them. He was close. Very close. At least that's what he thought.

So, he asked around and someone gave him the location of Lester and Henry's home. Daddy went looking for it and finally found them living north of Lake Minti. As if by chance, he dropped in and made their acquaintance, once again. Then, over the better part of six months, Calvin's daddy got to know those old-timers better and better. He would personally deliver his moonshine to their cabin and spend time talking. All three of them would gather round and share stories while drinking lots of his brew. Slowly, ever so slowly, Daddy gained their trust. He planned to feed them enough liquor to get all the details of the gold mine and then he would go steal their gold. It might take him awhile, but he was determined to get what he wanted.

Well, eventually, Calvin's daddy had learned quite a lot about these two old-timers. They truly believed that they had found a new friend in him, so they began to open up. That was just fine with Daddy. He believed that he was finally on that road to getting rich. Now, Daddy wasn't much of a gold digger, but he definitely could use the money. He'd have to figure a way to dig up the gold once he got the necessary information. But that was all right - that would be the easy part.

Daddy took Calvin on several of these trips to the old-timers' cabin. Woodrow wasn't ever invited. Calvin was smarter than Woodrow and he knew when to be quiet, how to look innocent, and when to say something that would help his daddy. So Calvin was used to help get information from the old-timers.

Daddy had learned a lot about this gold mine. He learned that one of the old-timers had heard about the legend from one of his grandfathers. The grandfather had learned of the legend from the son of one of the original prospectors. Daddy learned that there was truth to the legend and he found out that the old-timers had a pretty good idea of the gold mine's location.

The part that he couldn't manage to get out of them was the exact location of the gold mine. He also wanted to know why the two old-timers didn't just go get the gold for themselves. And, while he was asking questions, was the gold still there and who else had they told?

It finally reached a point one day, when Daddy had grown real tired of going to see Lester and Henry each and every week. He had developed a friendship with them through his regular visits and deliveries of his special whiskey. They seemed to love the free whiskey. But, despite all of this goodwill, Daddy couldn't get the last remaining pieces of information out of them. So he decided to change his strategy once again. The old-timers had developed a fondness for the boy and Daddy knew it. So, Daddy decided to use Calvin as bait. He told the two men that Calvin was sick and needed some expensive medical procedures.

"Just like fishing," Daddy told Calvin, "When the fish ain't biting, its time to change the bait."

Who said Daddy wasn't a great fishing guide? He had found the fish. His timing seemed to be right. All he had to do was change his bait – and he did.

All he had left to do after that was reel to them in. And, reel the old-timers in, he did.

He told them that Calvin was dying of some rare mountain disease. Yes, he knew that Calvin looked all right, but that was one of the terrible traits of this mountain disease - the victim looked just fine. Then suddenly, without warning, the victim would just go to sleep one night and never wake up again. It was a terrible disease, he mournfully informed them.

It was a terrible lie. One that never should have been told.

But it *was* told. And Daddy told it.

Calvin was instructed ahead of time to just sit there and smile. Daddy told the old-timers that the disease was spreading inside Calvin and, any day now, he expected to wake up one morning and find his poor, dear, sweet son fast asleep – permanently.

Daddy proceeded to pour the old-timers a little bit more whiskey while Calvin smiled innocently. Daddy sat back and waited for them to ask what they could do to help.

They finally did.

"You know, we just hate to see the poor boy not get the help that he needs," said Lester.

"He seems to be such a nice boy," said Henry.

"I bet they wouldn't help him in Prospect," commented Lester.

Daddy had to resist the urge to ask them about Prospect. He bit his lip and calmly waited.

"You know, you're right. Just look at him. I can see how he's starting to waste away," observed Henry.

"I wish there was something we could do about it," Lester remarked.

This was exactly the moment that Daddy had been waiting for.

He was prepared. He told them that he needed money for an operation - an expensive operation. But if that wasn't enough bad news, Daddy would need even more money for the pills, those costly medications that he would have to buy to keep Calvin from having a relapse.

They understood that it would take a lot of money.

Then Daddy told them that he didn't want their money (which he believed they didn't have much of anyway) but rather, if they knew of a place where he could find money – or something just like money, like oh, say gold – then he wouldn't mind doing all the work of finding it and digging it up and transporting it and selling it. He told them that he didn't mind doing the work, as long as it would save his poor, dear, sweet son's life. Then he tried real hard to get misty eyed.

He told them that he didn't care how far away the gold was. He loved his son so much, that he would do this all by himself and not bother the generous old-timers anymore.

They bought it, almost as fast as you could say, "Fort Knox."

* * * * *

We left the Nature Center at closing time and left a message for Mr. Baker that we would be back tomorrow to finish our tour. We had a great dinner at a Mexican restaurant, went to our hotel and watched TV. Katie and Uncle Steve fell asleep quickly. I was anxious for Amy to return, which probably kept me awake. Amy tiptoed into our room around ten o'clock.

Amy was thrilled to hear about Sarah and wanted to know everything that happened. We talked for a whole hour. Amy was particularly interested in hearing how Sarah recovered by eating the plant. I was so excited that my voice would get louder, and twice we nearly woke up Uncle Steve. He snorted, smacked his lips together, then rolled over in his bed and kept on sleeping. Amy was greatly relieved and assured me that everything seemed to be fine now. We were both very tired and agreed to talk more after seeing Sarah the next day. We drifted off to sleep. I dreamed of Sarah.

The next morning, Amy was up and out the door before eight o'clock. The rest of us took our time. We packed our clothes, watched some TV, and had breakfast at Cracker Barrel. I like Cracker Barrel. Their food is real good and the people are always so nice. I played that game that they have on each table. You know the one I'm talking about - the one with the triangle stand and the different colored golf tees? The goal is to jump over your own golf tees and play it so you only have one golf tee remaining. I usually end up with three or four left, which isn't bad. Once, I even got down to one.

Since we were planning on meeting Mr. Baker at ten o'clock, we went directly over to the Center. Mr. Baker was going to share some more information with us and then we would get to see the raptor habitat. By that time, Amy's class would be over. Then we would pick up Sarah and Amy and go back to Mountview. Sounded like a pretty good day. I was very happy that Sarah was doing so much better.

I was looking forward to talking with Mr. Baker. Amy had spoken very highly of him and said that he had a lot of experiences that we would find very interesting.

We met at the main desk and were escorted to Mr. Baker's office, which was down the hall, past the restrooms and water cooler, then off to the right.

"So, have you enjoyed your visit?" Mr. Baker inquired.

"Absolutely. It was great. My favorite is Carrie the Cougar," Uncle Steve replied.

"I like the snakes," Katie said proudly.

"Nocturnal Hall was great. Caruso is awesome. I enjoyed listening to Mr. Dill's stories. I like the one about hoop snakes," I said.

"Oh yes, the good old hoop snake." Mr. Baker nodded. "Of course you are referring to the snake that makes a big wheel with his body when he bites his own tale, and can roll down hills. Yes, that's a good one. We hear some funny things. Not only myths, like the hoop snakes, but we get to see a lot of very interesting things that nature has provided. For example, I have seen a two-headed turtle; we've had a couple of albino snakes…"

"I like snakes," Katie interrupted.

"I'm glad to hear that, Katie; most people don't like snakes. As a matter of fact, some people feel that they need to kill any snake they see. It's a shame. Nature has lost a lot of good snakes due to ignorance. Snakes are part of the ecosystem. When we move into their space, they have nowhere to go. So they hang out with us. What do they expect will happen? People are scared – they're ignorant, so they kill the snakes.

"We see that people are very intolerant of nature. They always want a magic pill that will scare away all the snakes, or all the skunks, or raccoons. As humans consume more and more forest and fields, we **cannot** expect all the animals just to go away. Some will go away and just may go away forever, which would be a very bad thing. Some others won't go away. We try to bridge that gap and try to educate people as to why that animal is there and to tell them why that animal won't hurt them. It is very hard to deal with fear and ignorance. So we educate. We seem to serve a valuable purpose that way. We won't always make people happy, but we will always give them factual and true information."

"And how do you do that?" asked Uncle Steve.

"Well, first we are open almost everyday of the year. So the public can come in and get acquainted with their animal friends. Education first starts with familiarity. We have a hands-on Nature Lab and Educational Farm with a petting area. In our facility, we have invited children to touch a corn snake, hold a turtle, and feel real angora, pre-sheared. We also offer classes to the public so that they can learn more about the world around them. Many of our staff are recognized as regional specialists and serve as consultants to zoos and other wildlife habitats. So we know what we are talking about. And then we have programs such as our Junior Naturalist Volunteer Program, which gives children between the ages of twelve and fifteen an opportunity to really expand their knowledge of wild and domestic animals."

"That's what I'm going to join," I proudly announced.

"Good for you, Austin," Mr. Baker said.

"Me too!" Katie piped in, flipping her blond curls away from her eyes.

Mr. Baker smiled, "Well, I appreciate your enthusiasm, Katie, so when you turn twelve years old, we will have a place waiting for you. We also have special events each month that are posted on our calendar and we have some extra special events such as a 'Wolf Howl' where we invite guests to come and learn more about the red and gray wolves of North America. The group is treated to a real 'Wolf Howling' at the wolf habitat."

"We heard those howls and they are scary," Katie said.

"How about a Wolf Howl-o-ween party?" I suggested.

"See, there you go - a natural marketer," Mr. Baker smiled. "I will have to tell Greg Murdock about your gift for marketing.

"We have a very special place around here. I am not just talking about our Nature Center. I mean this whole part of the country. The Appalachians are one of the oldest mountain chains in the world. People from all over the world come here to study. The salamander population in the Appalachians is the most diversified in the whole world. Did you know that salamanders are able to regenerate their limbs and even regenerate their eyes?

"If a salamander loses a leg, it can grow one back. We have witnessed a Hellbender who lost an eye, regenerate another eye. That is truly remarkable! Scientists travel from all over the world to watch and study this phenomenon in hopes that medicine, some day, will be able to do the very same thing. Just think of being able to regenerate limbs and to be able to regenerate eyes. Isn't that truly remarkable? That's why we are here - to improve life not only for people but also for our animal friends."

Then we heard it.

"EEEKKK!"

And then we heard another, even louder, scream.

"EEEKKK!"

We all looked in the direction of the screams. They came from down the hall.

Mr. Baker jumped up from his desk and headed for the hallway. We quickly followed.

A lady in a blue-flowered dress came flying out of the bathroom, almost smashing into another lady with red hair like a beehive, who was leaning against the wall and shaking like a leaf.

"Something is in there...." panted the beehive lady, pointing to the closed bathroom door. "It's gross. Something is in there. Oh…"

Mr. Baker put his hand against the bathroom door. Before he entered he asked, "Is it an animal, a snake, or a bug? Can you describe it? Did something hurt you?"

The flower lady, who was now also leaning on the wall gasped, "It looks like that thing may have been an animal at one time, but I don't know what it is now. It's so slimy. It's so ugly. It was going to eat me. Oh…"

"Yes, but are you both all right?" Mr. Baker asked them again.

"Yes, I'm fine. I got out just in time. It was going to eat me, too!" the flower lady insisted.

"OK, OK. I'll take care of it. Just relax," Mr. Baker reassured the two women.

He then looked around the hallway and noticed that I was closest to him. "Austin, whatever you do, don't open this door until I give you a sign."

My eyes got real big. "What kind of sign?"

"I don't know," Mr. Baker admitted. "How about, 'you can open the door now?'" Then he slowly opened the door. The light was off. The bathroom was black.

The beehive lady exclaimed, "See! That thing ate the light, too!"

Mr. Baker looked at her, then flipped the light switch on. Light filled the room. Mr. Baker slid through the narrow, open door.

"I must have hit it on the way out," the flower lady nervously admitted to the rest of us.

The door closed behind Mr. Baker. We heard rustling. Something hit the ground - I thought it was Mr. Baker. There was more rustling. Then there was silence. I wanted to open the door, but didn't.

Finally we heard, "You can open the door now."

I slowly pushed the door open.

There was Mr. Baker on his knees. His cap was now crooked. His clothes were wet, dirty and wrinkled and, in his arms, was the most grotesque looking thing I have ever seen. I could see why the women were screaming.

It was that nasty Eastern Hellbender!

Mr. Baker slowly stood up. He was very careful not to hurt the Eastern Hellbender. I held the door open as he exited the bathroom.

Out in the hall, Mr. Baker was smiling, holding the scared animal securely and said, "I am terribly sorry, ladies, for this inconvenience. This fellow won't hurt you. This guy is not poisonous, he won't bite, he doesn't breathe fire, and he definitely won't eat you. Let me introduce you to our Eastern Hellbender."

Mr. Baker handed it to one of his staff members and said, "OK, I think we need to fix the Hellbender habitat. This boy escaped and will do it again unless we fix the pen - please do it right away and thank you, Jim."

Then he turned to the two gawking women. "I'm so sorry, ladies. The bathroom is now officially reopened," Mr. Baker announced, smiling. "Please let me know if there is anything else we can do for you." He looked at his soiled shirt and said to us, "Why don't we head back to my office? I'll join you as soon as I clean up."

We went back into Mr. Baker's office. There never seems to be a dull moment around this place.

Mr. Baker entered the room, buttoning a clean shirt. "Let me tell you about that guy, the Eastern Hellbender. You may know of him through one of his other names - the Allegheny Alligator, Devil Dog and the Mud Cat."

Mr. Baker took his seat behind his desk and continued. "The Hellbender is one of the largest salamanders in the world. It's nearly two and one-half feet long and can weigh as much as five pounds. They live in cool streams that are one to three feet deep, with large rocks scattered on the bottom. That big tail propels them. They range in color from that brown you saw to bright orange or red. They are extremely slimy, which makes them very difficult to catch. But it probably serves the purpose of keeping them free from infections and from being eaten. They are ugly, but not dangerous. If you know of a good trout stream, chances are there are also Hellbenders there. Many of the rivers that still contain high numbers of Hellbenders are surrounded by undeveloped land, like National Forest. As our cities and suburbs begin to spread out farther and farther into the countryside, the health of these streams will continue to decline and so will our Hellbender population. It is a threatened species.

"As far as that guy, he was just laying next to the toilet. It was cool and quiet and safe. At least until those ladies started screaming. He was probably more scared than the ladies."

"He sure is one ugly animal," Uncle Steve observed.

"Yes, he is, but to a female Eastern Hellbender he is downright handsome." Mr. Baker smiled.

We laughed. "Of course, he managed to get out and where did he go? To the worst possible place he could go - the women's restroom! Although I don't think he meant to terrorize." Mr. Baker shook his head. "Now, where were we?"

"I believe we were talking about symbiotic relationships - animal relationships with humans," Uncle Steve said.

"Ha, we weren't really there, were we? Oh you mean…" His voice trailed off as he pointed to the hall where we had just seen the Hellbender. "Yeah, now that truly is a symbiotic relationship. Speaking of ugly animals, did you guys, excuse me, Katie, did you all see the vultures?" Mr. Baker inquired.

"I believe it's a tossup for the ugliest creature - Hellbender vs. vulture," I commented.

"Ugly they are, but did you know that they are key players in nature's clean-up crew? One of our education specialists, Tracy Trout, wrote a great article about the vulture."

He picked up the article and read, "From a distance, soaring effortlessly in circles high above our heads, the vulture is arguably the most graceful and agile of birds. But they have some disgusting habits."

"Like what?" I interrupted. This sounded cool.

"Well, their diet consists of carrion. That is dead flesh," Mr. Baker informed us.

"Eeeewww," Katie groaned.

"They excrete on themselves," Mr. Baker added.

"Eeeewwww," Katie repeated.

"They vomit when nervous or faced with danger," Mr. Baker said.

That got another "Eeeeewww" from Katie.

"Sounds like one of the guys in my gym class," I joked.

Mr. Baker chuckled. "And, let's face it, they are downright ugly. But after you get past all of that, you have to appreciate what nature has given us. As scavengers, they are essentially nature's clean-up crew, quickly removing carcasses from the landscape before they rot and turn foul. Now do *you* want to do that, or would you rather have something else do that for you?"

We all agreed – that was an excellent point.

"Vultures can even eat diseased meat and not get sick themselves. Studies have shown that the disease organisms do not survive once passed through a vulture's digestive system. Therefore, they help prevent the spread of disease," Mr. Baker said. "So, the next time you see a vulture, don't harm it, but appreciate it for the job it is doing for you."

Once again, we all agreed – another great point!

"I have a question. Mr. Murdock said that the gray wolf and the cougar were the most aggressive predators. But now they're all gone, what happens when they leave?" I asked.

"Good question," Mr. Baker said approvingly. "Let me start by saying that an integral part of a healthy ecosystem is having animals preying on other animals. I know that sounds terrible, but it is nature and it is a natural thing that takes place in our world. Preying on other animals is an extremely important activity because that usually takes out the weaker member of the herd, which keeps the gene pool stronger, and makes for healthy ecosystem and keeps a balanced population between predator and prey. That is one of Mother Nature's goals and it helps us maintain a healthy and balanced environment.

"So, when the biggest predator becomes extinct, or in this case the two biggest predators become extinct, in order to balance nature another predator will move into the area. That is why the coyotes have moved into this area. They are not native; they have moved in to fill this void where the Eastern cougar, gray wolf, and red wolf used to dominate. A gray wolf hasn't been documented in the Southeast since the early nineteen hundreds. Same with the cougar. Mostly because of bounties placed on them by settlers since they were a threat to their livestock. So now we have coyotes in the Carolinas."

"Another question: I was reading about the cougar, or mountain lion, that it always attacks from behind. People don't see them coming. Is that right?" I wondered.

"Well, I don't know if 'always' is the right word. But we do know that it is a preferred way to hunt prey - primarily because cats like to hunt. They like the chase, which means that they capture most of their prey when the prey is trying to run from them with their backs to the cats. So, yes, they capture from behind. That reminds me of a story that I heard. The India tiger is one of the most powerful animals on our planet. I heard that in an estuary area where villagers would frequently go for food and water, the tiger would sit there and wait for them. When the villagers were getting water from the pool, the tigers would invariably attack them. The villagers determined that the tigers didn't attack when the villagers faced the tigers. It seems that the tigers would never attack head on. Well, the villagers weren't allowed to kill the tigers, since they are a protected species. So what were the villagers going to do?" Mr. Baker asked, waiting for us to respond.

"What *did* they do?" Katie was first to ask.

"Well, the villagers got this great idea to put facial masks on the back of their heads when they were collecting oysters or water or something out in the marsh. So, when tigers would creep up in the very tall grass behind them, the tigers would see their faces and wouldn't attack. This brilliant move stopped the tigers from killing the villagers," Mr. Baker concluded.

"Wow!" I exclaimed. That was definitely very cool.

Chapter 8

The old-timers had believed Daddy and they didn't want to see Calvin suffer. So they gave Daddy the valuable information he had been searching for.

The old-timers revealed that the hole-in-the-mountain was real. And, as the legend stated, there was a golden statue guarding the entrance to an old, Spanish gold mine.

They also told Daddy that the gold mine was located in Waynesville Cliffs. Although Waynesville Cliffs was a big place, the mountain where the so-called hole was located was easily identifiable because the top of that mountain was flat - very uncharacteristic for mountains in the Appalachians. What was even more uncharacteristic was that on top of that mountain, among the towering hardwood trees, was a field of golden plants with red berries on them, thriving in that rich, black soil. There wasn't another field like that anywhere in the Southeast. Since the yellow, golden plants were so bright, when the early morning sun shined through the tall hardwoods, it was like a beacon – shimmering golden plants waved their bright red berries in the morning sun, tempting anyone within sight to come visit them.

They also told Daddy that this particular mountain was very dangerous. The paths were either completely blocked by fallen rocks or were very narrow and extremely treacherous. If someone was unfortunate enough to slip from the paths, the fall was very far and most deadly.

Daddy listened to every word. He was thrilled! But there were still a few unanswered questions and Daddy was determined to get all the answers he could. "So, why didn't you go get the gold yourselves? Was it because you heard there was a curse on it?"

"We wanted the gold," Henry said. "Yeah, we heard that there was a curse on the gold, but we didn't believe in curses. We did go after it, many, many years ago, when we were much younger. We tried several times and, I am sorry to say, we lost some of our friends in those attempts. One fell off the mountain. Another friend just turned up missing one morning – we never found him. And another shot himself by mistake…at least that's what we believed."

Lester added, "See, we needed the money back then, but, after losing so many friends, we became afraid of the curse. You know, we started believing that the curse was real."

Daddy jumped in. "So you just left it there and never returned? How could you just walk away from so much money?"

"We figured we were just lucky not to have been killed ourselves," Henry explained. "We didn't want to tempt fate. So we thought it was best to keep the secret and not tell anyone."

"So you never told anybody? No one else knows the location?" Daddy asked excitedly, not daring to believe he was so lucky.

"That's right," Lester nodded. "We figured it was best kept a secret. Plus, there was this real estate developer over in Prospect who really wanted Henry's family farm. He ended up given Henry a bunch of money for it. Matter of fact, he got a ton of money. Those developers are crazy and just don't seem to know when to quit."

Henry chuckled. "This here developer came up here to see us one day and tried to get me to sell the family place. We could see that he was real interested and we just wanted to see how much he was willing to pay. It got to be a game for us. He started coming over all the time, as if he was trying to become our good friend. We knew what he was up to. So all we did was sit there and tell stories every time he came by. He would sit and act real interested and try not to yawn. It was downright funny watching him sit through all our boring stories. We knew he was going to buy our property and, every time he came by, he would raise his price a little. And we would turn him down every time. Ha!

"Well after awhile, we began to feel sorry for this poor fellow. So the next time or two he came by we told him that we would sell. We ended up with all the money we would ever need."

Lester jumped in. "So what's the use in trying to get that gold? We're too old to spend that much money. We don't have any kin who could use it. And we just don't need it. So why should we go all the way there for something we won't ever need?"

Daddy was too busy thinking about getting rich to answer the question. He was also too busy to realize that he had been played just like the real estate developer. He had also stopped thinking of what other questions he should ask the old-timers. He was blinded by greed.

Now, what Daddy neglected to ask the old-timers was if the golden statue was the only thing guarding the entrance to the mine. If he had asked them, they would have told him that the mine was also guarded by a pack of Eastern mountain lions, which had lived in the hole for a very long time. So the legend was correct about that, as well.

Another question that Daddy didn't ask was about were those golden plants that grew on the top of the mountain. The old-timers would have told him to stay away from them…that the plants were deadly. If you touched them, you could transfer the juice to your mouth, or it could seep through your skin. If anyone ate the stalk or the leaves of those plants, they would die. If anyone ate the berries from that plant, they would become very sick. They had seen it happen. They knew what they were talking about.

But Daddy had all the information that he needed…at least, so he assumed. He didn't believe in curses and he knew that he could go get this gold and now he knew exactly where to find it. He was all set…he thought.

After some brief goodbyes, Daddy told Lester and Henry that he needed to leave immediately so that he could find the gold, before it was too late.

Henry asked Daddy, "So, where will you be taking Calvin?"

Daddy, in his haste, wasn't thinking clearly and answered, "Calvin, what do you mean, where will I take Calvin?"

Lester asked, "Where will you take the boy to get his operation?"

Daddy quickly remembered his lies. "Oh, the operation! Oh yes. Well, Calvin will need to go to, uh…Charlotte. As soon as I find the gold, then we'll take Calvin to the hospital there…in Charlotte."

"When you go after the gold, will Calvin go with you?" asked Henry.

"Oh no, no," Daddy replied. "He won't be going with me for that…too dangerous for the kid. Hey, look at the time," he said, looking at his watch. "We have to be going. Yeah, we got to go. Thanks for everything. See you later." And with that, Daddy grabbed Calvin and they were gone.

About a mile down the road, Daddy began laughing and laughing. He was sure he had reason to be laughing because he had outsmarted the old-timers. He figured that he had just swindled two dumb old men and now he was going to get rich. That was what he thought.

After Daddy and Calvin left, Henry asked Lester, "Why didn't you tell him everything?"

"Why didn't you?" countered Lester.

"Well, it seemed that Daddy had a lot on his mind. I didn't want to make it any more difficult for him. If he can figure it all out, then he deserves the gold," Henry said.

"Plus, you know that nice kid of his isn't really sick?" Lester asked, shaking his head.

"Oh I know that. I just didn't want that nice kid to get caught up in the mountains with his idiot daddy. And, while we're talking about it, why would someone want to be called 'Daddy?' Especially by people who aren't his kin?" wondered Henry, scratching his beard.

"You know, Daddy is a liar and a cheat. All he wanted was to take something that didn't belong to him," Lester stated.

"Plus, his whiskey wasn't really that good," Henry observed.

"But it *was* free," Lester laughed.

Henry added, "I still say we could have gotten another month of liquor out of him. He was greedier than that real estate developer." He paused for a moment. "He deserves everything he gets."

"Good luck there, Daddy. You are certainly going to need it," Lester said wryly, waving goodbye to the cloud of dust left by Daddy's rapidly departing car.

Well, Daddy never did get a chance to use that information. But he did deserve everything he got coming to him…and then some.

Shortly after getting all the information about the gold mine from the old-timers, Daddy got caught for the third time by the State Alcohol, Tobacco, and Firearms Police for transporting illegal liquor. After his arrest and trial, Daddy ended up going to the Perry Correctional Institution in Columbia to serve his five-year (but three-with-good-behavior) sentence.

That's when things really became hard for Momma. She had to finish raising Calvin and hoped that Woodrow could figure out a way to put food on the table. But Woodrow couldn't provide for the family; he just didn't know how to do that. So Calvin dropped out of school to hunt and he occasionally found work as a fishing guide. Calvin was now responsible for his family.

After a full year, Calvin, the smart Garner, decided enough was enough. He turned his attention to another matter. He could either wait for Daddy to get out of prison and then they could go find the gold together, or he could go get the gold all by himself. After all, he figured, he was just as smart as Daddy, and maybe even smarter, considering that he was still free and Daddy was locked up for five years (but three with good behavior). Who needed Daddy, a convicted felon, around anyway?

So that was when Calvin decided it was his turn to be somebody. Who said he wasn't ambitious? He knew that he could be a great gold miner. Of course, he would be a miner only as long as it took to find the gold. Or as long as it took him to take the gold from the person who did find it. He didn't care. He needed the money and he would take it from wherever it was, or from whoever had it.

He started developing a plan.

Calvin became real neighborly, as they say up there in Spencer. He began talking to people around town and getting them to tell him everything they knew about the Waynesville Cliffs. He told people that he was going to offer guided trips in and around Prospect. He told them that he needed to get information about the entire area. So it was natural for him to be asking about The Cliffs.

The town folk, there in Spencer, were downright pleased to have Calvin take an interest in their town and their area. They felt sorry for the boy whose father abandoned him, got locked up, and left him to care for his momma and his brother. Calvin liked the attention he was getting.

He liked the information even better.

* * * * *

Mr. Baker looked at his watch and said, "You'd better be going now. This has been fun. But, before you go, there's one more person I would like you to meet. She's a very interesting person who, like most of us, wears a lot of hats around here. Her name is Leslie Ann Fisher. She is one of our rehabilitators and she is also an animal communicator."

That really got my attention. "You mean she can talk to the animals?" I asked.

"Yes, that is exactly what I mean." Mr. Baker paused for a moment. "Don't look so shocked. What our Nature Center tries to tell people is that animals are complex creatures. The animal kingdom uses a complex system of communication. Do you think humans know everything? Far from it, we know so very little. Our goal is to help teach people - our visitors - about animals with the hope they will learn and respect the animals. There is so much for us to know. We have only scratched the surface of our knowledge about our own planet. But this is a start. You will enjoy meeting Leslie Ann. However, you don't have a lot of time. You will need to make a choice between seeing Leslie Ann or seeing the raptor habitat. What do you want to do?"

I looked at Uncle Steve and Katie. "I'd like to visit Leslie Ann."

Katie, of course, said, "I want to see the raptor thing." I told you, we had been spending way too much time with each other.

"Austin, I know you will want to talk to Leslie Ann so why don't you go see her," Uncle Steve proposed. " I'll escort Katie to the raptor habitat. Is that OK with you?"

Definitely.

Leslie Ann's office was one floor below us. Mr. Baker gave me the directions. In a minute, I was standing in her office.

I introduced myself, and Leslie Ann said that Mr. Baker had called her to let her know I was on my way.

Leslie Ann was attractive, probably in her early forties. She had wavy, dark hair, which she kept combed back. She was about Amy's size and she spoke with a very soft voice. She began our discussion by telling me how the Western North Carolina Nature Center acquires their animals.

The first way is that they are part of a larger organization called the AZA, or the American Zoo Association. The AZA interacts with all the zoos: they trade animals, exchange helpful information, share research, and work with each other closely.

Another way is through rehabilitators – she's one of those. It seems that some animals come from captive breeding and local wildlife. Rehabilitators bring in animals that can't be released due to disorders such as missing eyes, broken wings, or being imprinted. If these animals were released, they would cause further injury or death to themselves. Since they are so used to being around human beings and aren't afraid of us, they would probably scare everybody by coming right up to us.

She gave me an example using bears. It seems that bears take their first two years to learn from their mother. If a bear is raised in captivity, then their mother hasn't been teaching them, so they are at a distinct disadvantage if released into the wild. Instead of releasing the bears into the wild, where they would probably die an early death, the bears live in a protective zoo, such as The Western North Carolina Nature Center, until they die. This is much better than any other alternatives. Leslie Ann said that each spring a Rehabilitator course is taught and a license is given to work with local mammals, reptiles, and non-migratory birds.

"Please tell me about talking to the animals," I requested as nonchalantly as I could under the circumstances.

Leslie Ann began, "I would like to share with you a very personal experience I had with our female cougar, Carrie. One morning as I approached the cougar habitat, I noticed Carrie coming out of her night house at an unusually slow pace. Normally, she would lunge forward at full speed in anticipation of getting breakfast. As I got closer to her to get a better look, she got into a crouched position and began a deep gurgling cough, which lasted for an extended period of time. I knelt down beside her, anxious for her to get her breath. Finally, she stopped coughing and by now I was almost nose-to-nose with her. When she raised her head and her eyes met mine, these three words popped into my mind: Please help me."

"You mean, like she sent those words to you?" I asked, trying to contain my excitement.

"Yes. At the same time that I visualized her words, I heard a soft and beautiful voice saying those very same words. I also felt the words deep in my chest, right here where my heart lies. The experience was one of seeing, feeling, and hearing all at the same time. I immediately responded by verbally telling her, 'I will get help for you today.'"

"I know what you're talking about," I stated.

Leslie Ann looked at me quizzically, then continued. "I located the animal curator and informed him of her condition and he contacted the vet to have her seen at once. She received a shot of antibiotics and a prescription for oral medication. She was given the diagnosis of respiratory infection. I had to help out in another work area that afternoon, but before leaving at five o'clock, I went back to check on Carrie.

"As I neared the entrance door to her night house and called to her, she got out of her bed and came over to me, quietly laying down beside me and rolling over on her back. She looked at me and, as our eyes met once more, she gave me a great big beautiful smile that was literally ear-to-ear.

I knew she was saying thanks. After finishing her medication, she had a full recovery. Now she is back to her old self again."

"That's a great story!" I exclaimed. "So there *are* people who can really talk with the animals!"

"Oh yes. There are quite a few people that I have met who have that capability. So, do you believe that you can talk with the animals?" she asked.

"Yes, ma'am, I believe I can," I admitted. I realized that I felt very comfortable talking with Leslie Ann. I decided to tell her several secrets.

I told Leslie Ann how I could send messages to Sarah, my pet skunk. I told her that I've been working with Dr. Dixon. He has a new technique that will help me expand my sending capabilities. It's called 'imagery' and we have been busy practicing it. Since Leslie Ann and I both send to animals, she suggested that we try to send to each other. We decided to try that when I was back home. I have never sent over such a great distance before, but I was up to the challenge. If Dr. Dixon's techniques work, then I will have solved the distance limitation.

"And what do the animals tell you?" Leslie Ann inquired.

"They tell me how they feel." I wasn't worried about trusting Leslie Ann. She seemed to be an honest person who truly believed in what she was doing. I liked her and we had something in common. "They tell me what they have been doing and what they plan on doing. They tell me what they like and what they are afraid of. I can't talk to all animals, just a few select ones."

"Those animals that you are close to, I would assume," she said.

"Yes, ma'am. But Dr. Dixon is helping me learn to send to him and, I hope, eventually, to other animals. I'm trying to do it without speaking out loud."

"Austin, animals tell us when they are lonely and when they want attention. Just watch a dog's tail when he sees you coming. He has missed you. Or, after you have been gone for a while, your dog will hardly let you out of his sight. He is telling you that he was lonely and that he doesn't want you to leave again. Those are signs that everybody can interpret. However, it takes a very gifted person to be able to 'hear' their dog, or 'hear' another animal 'sending' a message to you. So, you have that gift, do you, Austin? That is a very special gift indeed. I suggest that you practice with your doctor friend and see where it takes you. Not many people have your gift. Treasure it. Use it. And help others. That's what life is all about." She paused and looked at me.

"You just may have a tremendous gift, Austin. As you develop it, you may discover that your gift is a very powerful talent indeed. You will need to practice and share your gift with others. But also be very careful with whom you share your talent. You may find that this talent will enable you to communicate with many others. You may find that you can interpret thoughts before they are spoken and ideas before they are mentioned.

"I'm not saying this to frighten you, dear child. But if you truly have this ability at such an early age, then you must understand that as it develops, along with the gift will come responsibility. I can feel that you have a very strong presence here. Be careful, my young friend. Please stay in touch, Austin. Perhaps we can learn from each other."

"I hope you can come to our Nature Center in Mountview someday," I said.

"I would like to do that." Leslie Ann got up. "I really must be going, but it was wonderful talking with you. If you have any questions, don't hesitate to contact me. And, Austin, try contacting me without a telephone, OK?"

"Yes, ma'am," I promised.

I left her office and retraced my steps back to the lobby of the Center.

Wow!

As I walked through the halls and up the stairs, thoughts were racing through my mind. What had she just told me? My gift could develop into something very powerful? Did she say that? What else did she say? That I should be careful who I share this with. Well, that's what Dr. Dixon has been telling me all along. And what else did she say? Oh yeah, with the gift comes responsibility. What did that mean?

I found myself in the lobby. No one was there. I asked the cashier if she had seen Amy. She had, and directed me back to the Observation Room.

Amy was there with Mr. Baker and Sarah. Mr. Baker was holding Sarah and, much to my relief, she looked like her normal skunk self again. Mr. Baker confessed that he couldn't find a thing wrong with Sarah and that she looked and acted perfectly fine. "See what a trip to the Western North Carolina Nature Center will do for somebody…and some animals?"

We laughed.

Boy, was I relieved. We thanked Mr. Baker for his time and the great tour by his staff.

We were soon joined by Katie and Uncle Steve. We invited Mr. Baker and his staff to Mountview to see our Center and he said that we would do that someday. Amy was ready to go. Sarah went back into her cage and then we all left the fabulous Nature Center. I can't wait to come back one day and see all the animals and my new friends.

Our ride back was definitely different than our ride there. Sarah was worn out from her ordeal; she was asleep in her cage. That was the same as before, only now, we all were relieved knowing that whatever had been wrong with her had been cured.

What we didn't know was *how* she had been cured. I told everybody about my incident with Sarah eating the plant and how Marcie nearly caught us. I mentioned that Sarah's ears were beginning to change back to her Schmooney ears just like her tail had changed back to a beaver. And then, after she ate the plant, she changed back to her skunk self, quickly.

I tried to describe the plant to Amy, but I couldn't remember enough details to give her an accurate description. Amy suggested that we catch up with Dr. Dixon when we were back home. If anyone would know, Dr. Dixon would know.

Uncle Steve asked me why Sarah couldn't tell us. I thought about that and figured that she might as soon as she gained her strength back. She was having trouble sending me messages, so I couldn't get any more answers. We all believed that she would be fine in a couple of days.

Katie told us all about the raptor habitat. I wish I could have seen it.

"Can we come back? I want to see the raptor habitat," I pleaded.

"Sure we can," Uncle Steve smiled.

Amy told us about several techniques that she learned from her meetings and shared with us several ideas on how to improve the Mountview Nature Center based on what other Centers were doing.

I decided to keep a lot of my conversation with Leslie Ann to myself. I shared her story about Carrie and everyone, including Katie, enjoyed it. But the rest of the stuff, the stuff about my gift becoming 'powerful,' I kept to myself.

So, considering everything that took place, we had a great time and were really happy that Sarah was on the road to recovery. We couldn't think of anything that would detract from our road trip. We figured that our future was bright.

We were almost correct.

What we didn't know was that things would get a lot worse before they got any better.

Chapter 9

Calvin was developing a plan that seemed to be workable. He knew his strengths and his weaknesses. One weakness was Woodrow, who was always getting into trouble and attracting unwanted attention. Although Woodrow was big and strong and older and all of those things, he needed supervision. What Woodrow really needed was an education, but Calvin just didn't have the time to give it to him. So he did the only thing he could with the limited time that he had - he supervised his older brother. He would give Woodrow jobs to do that kept him busy like cleaning equipment, taking care of their mother, cooking, and doing chores around the property. The sort of things that Calvin hated to do, that provided the additional bonus of keeping his brother out of trouble.

The problem was that Woodrow couldn't be watched all the time. Calvin wanted the boy to keep a low profile. He wanted to be respectable, at least for a while. He knew the information he was getting would stop flowing if the townspeople didn't trust him or his brother. So he needed to keep Woodrow quiet and safe – safe from himself.

But Woodrow always seemed to find trouble. Or maybe it was that trouble always found him. Like the times Johnny Bishop played jokes on Woodrow. Johnny Bishop was downright mean and nasty. He would pick on Woodrow, making fun of him in front of others, playing jokes on him, pushing him just far enough before Woodrow would get mad. Johnny wasn't stupid, so he would avoid pushing Woodrow too far. Remember, Woodrow was big - very big. Johnny was always trying to make himself look smart and brave by exploiting Woodrow's limitations in front of others.

There was a story about this one time when Johnny got a group of his friends together to play along with a joke he was planning. Johnny took an old funnel and put the end of it in the front of his pants so that the large part of the funnel was open and sticking out and the small end of the funnel was tucked into his pants under his belt. He then showed everybody that he had a quarter and put that quarter on his forehead, holding it there with his finger. Then he bent backwards. He then let go of the quarter, leaving it on his forehead, and extended both his arms out to his side, slowly raising his upper body. Gravity then caused the quarter to slide off his head and, if he did it just right, the quarter fell right into the funnel stuck in his pants. Johnny ended by standing straight up, with the quarter making a clinking sound as it hit the inside of the funnel. The crowd always applauded appreciatively. It was a cool trick.

Johnny planned this one carefully. He would show the trick to his group of friends and he would invite Woodrow to come see it. Now, the joke had everything to do with Woodrow. See, Johnny knew that if Woodrow saw the trick that Woodrow would want to try and show everybody that he, too, was cool and that he could be just like Johnny. So Johnny gave Woodrow a chance to show off by giving him the quarter and putting the funnel end firmly into the front of Woodrow's pants. Once Woodrow placed the quarter on his head and leaned backwards, extending his arms to the side, Woodrow would be unable to see what was going on in front of him – specifically, where the funnel was. Johnny, knowing this, reached behind a nearby tree and picked up a jug of water. While Woodrow was slowly straightening up, Johnny began to pour water into the funnel, which was still firmly wedged inside the front of Woodrow's pants.

Well, everybody started laughing. Johnny continued to pour water into the funnel. Woodrow was concentrating so hard on that quarter that he kept playing the game, totally unaware of what was going on. Johnny emptied the whole jug of water into Woodrow's pants. Everybody was laughing so loud that Woodrow must have thought they were excited for him. Woodrow even made the quarter slide off his forehead into the funnel.

Woodrow was extremely proud of himself, and looked around at the crowd for approval. It was right about that time that he realized something was wrong. He looked down to see that his blue jeans were soaked from his waist all the way down to his brown work boots. He was so wet that he was standing in a puddle of water. It took a moment for him to realize how he got so wet. He felt foolish. He noticed Johnny still holding the water jug and laughing. Laughing at him. Woodrow didn't like this at all. He wanted the jokes to stop once and for all.

They soon did.

That was the last time Johnny Bishop made fun of Woodrow. That was the last time anyone made fun of Woodrow, because that was the last time anyone saw Johnny. There were some questions asked, but there were never any answers given, and no trace of Johnny was ever found.

No one ever made fun of Woodrow again. Woodrow made it very clear that it wasn't nice to make fun of people.

As long as Woodrow didn't mess things up, I'll be fine, Calvin thought.

Calvin started planning his mining excursion at the bar one night. He had been talking to the deputy from Cherokee County who mentioned that the Golden Gato was getting some attention lately. Deputy Butch Larkin mentioned to Calvin that a newspaper fellow from Mountview, one Billy Johnson, was asking a lot of questions and gathering information for the Mountview Press.

"It seems that Billy has been asking about the local legends and his paper is planning on running a series about the history of Mountview," Deputy Larkin said during a casual conversation with his new friend, Calvin Garner.

Calvin knew about the hundreds, and perhaps thousands, of people who had searched the local area for the hole-in-the-mountain. When those new stories hit the newsstands, Calvin was sure that hundreds more would go out to try to find the gold. They would get in his way.

Some locals believed that the gold had already been found. But Calvin wasn't one of them. He knew that nothing had been found. Lester and Henry had convinced him of that.

He was sure that no one knew the Waynesville Cliffs area. And since it was so hazardous, as the old-timers told him, he was sure that no one but him would find it. Plus, now that he thought about it, it would take someone very familiar with the mountains to find the exact mineshaft. Someone not familiar with the area would run out of food and water before long, or might just fall off the pathway. And, if someone was up there while he was there, he would gladly assist in their 'accidental' fall off the pathway. The gold was still up there, just waiting for a smart fellow like Calvin to come claim it.

It was *his* gold! He would have it and he wanted it now!

But with all this talk and the newspaper about to run stories, the gold mine was going to get a lot of attention. Calvin wasn't worried about someone finding the mine. He was worried about someone finding him and his brother. Once he and Woodrow found the gold (and he knew he would find it), he would have to make multiple trips to get the gold back home and, he would need to make those trips unnoticed. That would be the problem. So he needed to find it fast. He just had to be ambitious and disciplined.

Deputy Larkin sure didn't present a pretty picture of what was up there in the mountains. Calvin could just taste the Golden Grotto, or whatever it was called. He knew that if it was there, he was going to get it. But the deputy confirmed everything that Lester and Henry had told him. It was dangerous. Rocks blocked most of the old paths. If anyone went up there, they would need to be a rock climber or have enough dynamite to blow the rocks away from the paths. Of course, using dynamite in an area that is known for rockslides would be crazy.

I may be crazy, thought Calvin, *but I will be crazy rich. The Golden Gallstone, or whatever it's called, is golden and I'm going to have it.* As Calvin joked to Woodrow, "This will be my golden moment." Unfortunately, Woodrow didn't get it.

Over the past three months, Calvin had been gathering all the tools that he would need for his trip to The Cliffs. He and Woodrow would need flashlights, hunting knives, shovels, a pickax, torches with fuel oil, a tent, sleeping bags, and a couple of sticks of dynamite for good measure. The dynamite was left over from the time his daddy used to fish.

He put as much food in a sack as he could, and packed his daddy's .357 pistol with a box of shells. He took only enough clothes to get him through a couple of weeks - he figured that he wouldn't be up there that long. He didn't care if he smelled. He would be rich. People didn't mind smelly people - as long as they were rich, smelly people.

Calvin had been gathering information for over three months now. Occasionally, he would see Lester and Henry. They would say hello, but they didn't get into any lengthy conversations. He had been asking different people, very discreetly, if they knew or had even heard about a unique mountain with yellow plants on the top. No one had ever heard of it. After a while, he began to doubt the story that Lester and Henry had told him.

But, between the conversations with the sheriff and the way people talk in their local bars, Calvin had a pretty good idea of where this unusual mountain was *not* located. Over the past decade, most people that had gone to the Cliffs never stayed there very long. Calvin had been there once. He and Woodrow had gone up there three months ago, just to look around. It was treacherous. He understood why people didn't go there. It wasn't that the mountain didn't exist; people just never wanted to go up there. But Calvin was smart. He knew that the gold would probably be in an area where no one had looked. It was definitely in Waynesville Cliffs. He knew how to get to the area; it was remote, and not easily accessible. There were dangerous paths and plenty of places for people to fall. Waynesville Cliffs seemed to be the very place a hole-in-the-mountain would be located.

Without raising suspicion, Calvin had asked his newfound friends at the county offices for area maps. He told them he was looking for hunting areas that were out of the way. They were all too pleased to help this poor boy whose father was in prison for five years (but three with good-behavior).

The time had come for Calvin and Woodrow to depart. Calvin told Woodrow to leave the house early one morning as if nothing special was going on. "Tell Momma that we will be gone for a couple of days, checking out some new hunting area. Don't tell her anything else."

Woodrow agreed.

So, that fateful summer morning, Calvin and Woodrow loaded their truck for the trip that would take them north as far as possible on SR 434. Then, they would make a left turn that would take them to Widows' Peak.

Once there, they would take the second dirt road on the right after the Esso Station. That dirt road led them to a dead end. It was at that specific spot on their map where the road stopped. Their map didn't give any more detail at that point. However, Calvin didn't need detail. He knew that was the specific spot where he could find the trail that would take them to the Cliffs – exactly where they needed to be.

When they arrived, they unpacked their gear, dividing everything into three duffle bags and two sleeping bags. Calvin took the lightest duffle bag, one of the sleeping bags, strapped his holstered .357 to his belt, and gave Woodrow the rest.

Calvin and Woodrow began climbing up the mountain, heading towards Waynesville Cliffs. They were on their way to incredible riches. They would be in the Cliffs tomorrow and they were excited. The gold had been there for over four hundred years, according to Lester and Henry. Calvin would see to it that the gold would be discovered and gone by the weekend.

He was looking forward to being somebody.

* * * * *

The next day Katie, Christina, and I were cleaning cages at the Nature Museum when we heard a car pull into the parking lot. The car's tires were making that distinctive deep, crunching sound tires make when they travel over gravel.

A car pulling into the Nature Museum parking lot was a common occurrence. But this one was special. I looked up and saw a bright red Ford pickup truck with Dr. Dixon getting out of the driver's side. In the bed of the truck was a long, thin boat, which looked like a canoe.

I waved and yelled, "Dr. Dixon!" He saw me and waved back. I wanted to talk to him and this was a perfect time. The cages could wait a few minutes. Katie and Christina followed me out to the front parking lot.

"Hello, Dr. Dixon, how are you?" I asked as I walked towards his truck.

I heard Katie say, "Buenos dias, Senor Dixon."

I stopped and slowly turned to look back at Katie. Katie and Christina had big smiles on their faces as they walked by me towards the truck. *This must be the new Katie,* I thought. *She can handle snakes and now she can speak Spanish. It appears that she is becoming her own person. I guess I'm just jealous.*

"Buenos dias, Katie y Christina," Dr. Dixon replied. "I didn't know you were such a good teacher, Christina. Do you think you could teach Spanish to an old fellow like me?"

"Dr. Dixon, you would learn quickly. You are a very smart person," Christina assured him.

"You know, I had forgotten that your mother is from South America. Your father, Keith, and I have known each other for some time now. He grew up just south of here."

"Yes, sir, my mother was born in Costa Rica, which is more like Central America," Christina politely reminded him.

"Yes, of course Central America. Costa Rica is a beautiful place. They say that the most beautiful women in the world are in Costa Rica, and, judging by your mother, they are right. That reminds me, next summer I will be going to Costa Rica for a conference. What is it like there?" Dr. Dixon asked.

"I have been there several times and I love it. The climate is mild, the people are so nice, and the country is a beautiful green," she responded.

"I want to go," Katie said. "Can I go with you, Dr. Dixon?"

"Hey, if anybody gets to go, it's me, right, Dr. Dixon?" I asked.

"Hold on, hold on, everybody. Mrs. Dixon and I are going to speak at a conference in the beautiful city of San Jose, Costa Rica. It's a world conference on rainforest preservation. But for you, it would be boring. We will be in a big room for several days with lots of people talking about preserving the rainforests and they won't let us leave to do anything and they probably won't feed us either. Now, who would like to go to that?" Dr. Dixon teased, trying to get us all to stop pestering him.

No one said anything for a moment.

Then Christina said, "I'll go." And that started it all over again. Katie and I were jumping up and down in front of Dr. Dixon. He finally said, "No, sorry. Not this time. Just me and Mrs. Dixon are going. Sorry." And that was that.

Dr. Dixon then noticed how wet and dirty Katie and Christina were. "If you don't mind me asking, how did you two get so dirty?" He motioned to their faces, shirts and pants, which seemed to all be the same color - white with brown splotches.

Katie looked down at her clothes, then at Christina's clothes and they noticed that their shirts and pants were covered with patches of dried mud. Their cheeks had brown streaks and there was straw in their hair. They pointed to the dirt on each other and started to laugh.

Dr. Dixon was shaking his head as if to say 'unbelievable.'

I laughed, too.

"Well, you are not so spotless yourself, Austin," Dr. Dixon observed.

I looked at the front of my pants and my shirt and I had to agree.

"I want to tell you all about the Western North Carolina Nature Museum," I said. "It was fantastic. And what made the trip so good is that Sarah is going to be all right. She ate some kind of plant on purpose and it made her feel better. Hey, what about that boat?" I pointed to his red truck.

"Whoa, whoa, you're going a million miles an hour. Let's slow down a moment," he suggested. "First, I know about Sarah - Amy called to tell me. You think I haven't been worried about her? I am delighted to know that she has recovered. But you have to tell me all about this mysterious plant. And, I do know about the Nature Center in Asheville. Didn't I tell you that you would find it interesting?"

"I like the snakes," Katie remarked, taking a break from her dirt. "They have a big green one over there that is real sweet."

"I'm sure they have a real sweet snake, Katie, and I'm sure you like them. Snakes and I made a deal a long time ago. We agreed that I don't mess with them and they, in turn, won't mess with me," Dr. Dixon said. "Now, I want you to tell me all about the snakes. And, Austin, I want to hear about your trip, too. But first, I want you to tell me everything about Sarah and this magical plant. How is my girl doing?"

"Amy thinks that she'll be just fine. She's still sleeping, you know, getting her strength back. She's inside the main building in the back room," I said, pointing to the largest, white building, which was next to us.

"Well, that's good to hear. I miss talking to her. Since everything is fine, I need to get some epoxy from Amy. I know she has a fiberglass repair kit in one of her storage sheds. I need to fix a hole in my kayak. Have you ever seen a kayak?" Dr. Dixon asked.

"No, I've heard about kayaks, but I've never actually seen one," I admitted, moving closer to his truck to examine its cargo.

"Well, look over there," Dr. Dixon instructed, pointing to his truck bed. "Now you have seen one. Come on over, by all means; all three of you need to come and see this truly amazing watercraft. It's the wave of the future."

"What is a kayak?" asked Katie.

"It looks like a canoe," Christina commented.

"Well, a kayak is a boat that was first used by the Eskimos. Yes, it does look like a canoe, but a kayak is more easily maneuverable, light to carry, waterproof - most of the time - warm, and fast for a paddle-driven craft. Kayaks range from five feet to thirty feet. This particular model is made out of fiberglass and seats one - me. I can store gear in the bow, up here," he pointed towards the front of the boat, "and in the stern, back here behind the seat." Then he picked up the back end of the kayak and added, "And, it's light enough for me to launch by myself."

"Wow, it's really cool. How fast can you go?" I wondered.

"Speed isn't the reason someone uses a kayak, Austin, but to answer your question, about the same speed as a canoe. The reason someone uses a kayak is for maneuverability and stealth. What I mean is that I can paddle into very shallow water or very deep water. I can paddle between rocks and through brush and I can do it all very quietly. For me, what's great about being on a kayak is taking pictures, observing wildlife, fishing, or just leisurely paddling."

"I like the color," Christina said.

"Me, too," Katie agreed.

"So, you took your kayak and paddled around Lake Minti today?" I asked.

"Oh, sure. Kayaks are fantastic. I can get into just about any area of the lake and I can do it very quietly. I took my camera and got some great pictures. I need to take the film to Fowler's Drug Store to get the pictures developed. Do you want to see them?" he asked.

"Sure do," we agreed simultaneously.

"Well, you guys finish your chores and I'll go find Amy and get that epoxy. It seems that this old kayak works a lot better when the holes are all fixed. I have a small leak in this one and need to patch her up. I think I bumped into a rock." Dr. Dixon paused for a moment. "Why don't you three come over later this afternoon? Austin, that will give me and you some time to talk about Sarah and this mysterious plant. I'll see if Amy has the time to drive you over. Mrs. Dixon was going to make some chocolate chip cookies - would you like some?"

We definitely agreed about that!

Dr. Dixon began walking towards the Center. I asked, "Dr. Dixon, with Sarah eating that plant and getting better, does that usually happen? Can you get better by eating a plant?"

"Oh, yes, of course. Many plants provide a natural cure to illness. Have you ever heard of a rainforest?" he asked.

"I've read about them," I replied.

"Lately, I've been catching up on my reading about rainforests. I believe the world is making a big mistake by not preserving our natural resources." He motioned towards the building. "Walk with me and I'll give you something to think about, young man."

We walked towards the main building. Katie and Christina headed back towards the cages to finish their work.

Dr. Dixon continued. "I have been active in spreading the word regarding the need to change the world's way of thinking about rainforests. See, the world is cutting down the rainforest trees and then using the land to farm. Did you know that the Amazonian Rainforest in South America covers over a billion acres, and includes areas in Brazil, Venezuela, Columbia, Ecuador and Peru? It is so large that if it were a country by itself, it would be one of the ten largest in the world."

He paused for a moment and looked at me. "But you didn't ask that question, did you? No, you didn't. I'm sorry. To answer your question, yes, plants offer cures for many illnesses. I'm not surprised that Sarah felt better by eating plants.

"We have learned a lot from the American Indians about plant cures. Folklore has passed down a wealth of information about natural cures. There are plants out there," he pointed towards the woods, "that will cure just about any disease known to man and, the rainforests offer many of these plants to the world.

"The cure to just about any disease is just sitting out there in the rainforests, waiting to be found by us. All we have to do is go find these cures." Dr. Dixon paused, perhaps to make a point, or maybe just to catch his breath. He seemed pretty excited about this topic. He continued. "Hopefully, those plants will still be there when we need them. If you are still interested and want to learn more, I'll look up some information and have it ready for you when you come by this afternoon. You *are* still coming by for Mrs. Dixon's cookies, aren't you?"

"Yes, sir. I am and that would be great," I assured him.

I watched Dr. Dixon walk towards the front door of the Nature Center. He stopped and looked back at me, then waved good-bye. I went back to help Katie and Christina finish cleaning the animal cages. My goal was to have every square inch of my clothes wet and covered in mud by the end of the day.

All three of us were well on our way to *that* goal.

Chapter 10

Meanwhile, the Waynesville Cliffs were becoming quite the gathering place. They had become the home of a couple of people who were already quite familiar with Sarah. Actually, they had previously met Austin, Katie, and Amy. They were bad men. Their names were Mr. Smith and Mr. Jones.

Apparently, Mr. Smith and Mr. Jones, who were last seen treading water in the pond on Mr. Dewitt Pickett's property, were very aware that they were wanted for kidnapping, assault with intent to cause bodily harm, leaving the scene of a felony, plus multiple EPA crimes-against-the-environment charges.

They knew that their old boss, Mr. Dewitt Pickett, formerly of Mountview, North Carolina, was about to do ten to twenty years of prison time in his new home at the Perry Correctional Institute in Columbia, South Carolina, and they wanted nothing to do with it or him.

So they did the only thing that people in their situation would do: they ran and ran and ran. Where they ended up wasn't that bad. They weren't quite sure where they were, but they had a nice cave for a home, a nearby pond that wasn't nearly as polluted as Mr. Pickett's, and the fish were easy to catch and tasted pretty good. On their way up to wherever they were, they did happen to 'borrow' some supplies from a local grocery store. So now, burglary and theft could be tacked onto their rapidly growing rap sheet.

They had enough food to last them for a while. Actually, Mr. Smith had enough Hostess Twinkies to last him another month or two, so he was happy. This place wasn't a Marriott, but it was safe and it would be home until the excitement died down. By the looks of things, no one ever came to this area. So they didn't have anything to worry about. All they had to do was to wait until things calmed down back in Mountview and Prospect and then they could slip away without anyone knowing about it. They would just bide their time and wait it out.

Mr. Smith and Mr. Jones were eating their normal breakfast. Mr. Jones was sitting on a rock inside one of the many caves in the cliffs, eating some Vienna Sausages right out of the can. Mr. Jones squeezed his big, fat fingers into the small opening in the can of sausages. He pulled one sausage out at a time with his fingers, placing one end of it in his mouth, then swallowing it in one gulp.

He looked over at Mr. Smith, who was sitting on the other side of their small fire. He stopped for a moment and observed Mr. Smith, who was reading an old newspaper, while stuffing Twinkies into his mouth. Mr. Jones watched Mr. Smith eat his Twinkie. There was a distinct pattern to his eating of the Twinkies, which had become almost a ritual. Mr. Smith would first nibble the top portion of the Twinkie, which would expose the cream center. Then, he would lick out the cream filling. Mr. Jones winced as he watched Mr. Smith shovel the cream filling down his throat. Then Mr. Smith would take the remaining part and cram it into his mouth in one bite.

Mr. Smith didn't do this just once. After eating the first one, he reached inside the paper bag, noisily removed another Twinkie, and did the same thing, all over again, following the exact same routine as before.

"Don't you ever get tired of eating those things?" Mr. Jones asked.

"No, these are great," Mr. Smith responded, white cream filling smeared all over his chin.

"You are disgusting," Mr. Jones pronounced.

"What do you mean? These are great!" Mr. Smith insisted.

Mr. Jones shook his head. "They may be great, but the way you eat them is disgusting. Wipe your face."

"Don't you have anything better to do than to watch me eat my breakfast?" Mr. Smith yelled as he wiped his chin with his sleeve.

There was silence and Mr. Smith went back to reading the paper. "It says here that there is going to be a movie made in this area. Movie scouts are coming to Prospect to make a movie up here. Ain't that cool! You want to be in the movies?"

"Movies? Be in the movies? Oh yeah, two good-looking guys like us are naturals. Right! Who is going to want us to be in movies?" asked Mr. Jones.

"I don't know. But I heard that they're always looking for new talent," Mr. Smith informed him. "And we definitely are new talent."

"They are always looking, you're right about that. And, while they're looking for movie sites, they might just find us. New talent, right! New talent willing to serve a ten-to- twenty-year-sentence, maybe." Mr. Jones stopped for a moment. "We need to go on another recon mission, to check out the area."

"How many recon missions do you need to take?" Mr. Smith asked, tossing his tattered newspaper aside "We've been here for three weeks and every day you make me go on a recon mission. Someone is going to see me 'reconning' around and we'll be in prison before you can say 'new talent!' We've been here for three weeks. How many people have you seen around here in those three weeks? Well, how many?"

Mr. Jones stared icily at Mr. Smith. "Look, even though I found this great place to hide, I just don't want someone to wander in here and catch us off guard or worse, catch you with a Twinkie in your face."

That reminded Mr. Smith that he hadn't finished his breakfast. "That's true," he admitted. "I would hate to have to share my Twinkies."

"Share my Twinkies…" Mr. Jones mocked, "Are you crazy? I don't want to share anything with anyone, especially share a jail cell with you."

Mr. Smith had finished his Twinkie. He looked up and now had cream filling on his nose. He remembered something that his partner had said. "What do you mean, *you* found this place? *I* found this place and you know it."

"You did not!" Mr. Jones insisted, reaching inside the can of sausages.

"I did too!" Mr. Smith persisted, with cream filling still on his nose.

"Did not!" Mr. Jones yelled, tossing his empty can into the fire.

"Did too, did too!" Mr. Smith shouted.

"You did, too!" Mr. Jones cried, changing tactics.

"I did not!" Mr. Smith unwittingly retorted.

"See, there you go - even you admit it!" Mr. Jones cackled triumphantly, pointing at a dumbfounded Mr. Smith. "OK, I'm going out to see what's out there." Mr. Jones rose. "Are you coming?"

They walked out of their cave, which was situated high within the Waynesville Cliffs. Mr. Smith had scouted the path leading east from where they were. The path led for about thirty yards and then ended abruptly at a rockslide that completely blocked their path. So they knew that there was nothing east of where they were that would give them any trouble.

Their cave faced north and, except for the wide, flat area just outside the cave, there was a drop-off that went a long way down. So they figured that no one would come from the north. Although there was the possibility of being seen from several other paths that were on the other side of the canyon below.

They had been west several times. The first was to cover their tracks. The other times it was just to make sure that no one was stumbling into the area.

That left south. That was a bit tricky. They didn't know what was behind them, but it was treacherous because the only path that led around their cave was partially covered with rocks. The drop-off from that path yawned beneath them, and neither one of them wanted to risk taking that route.

Therefore, they believed that no one else would attempt to negotiate that path either. They felt safe. But just to make sure, they ventured out of the cave and looked around outside. They saw rich green mountaintops, sculpted rock formations, and the sun coming up over the eastern crest. A slight breeze cooled their faces.

They weren't exactly appreciative of the majesty surrounding them. In fact, they couldn't have cared less. What they did care about was the mountain face, behind them. There was a path, but it was partially blocked. They decided that it looked as if it could get them around and up to the top. They both felt that they should check it out. But neither of them wanted to do it.

Today was no different.

* * * * *

Several hours after Dr. Dixon left, after the cages and pens were cleaned and the animals had their fresh water, after Katie and Christina had finished sweeping out the three main buildings, and, after I had painted the back door of Building Number Two, we were exhausted, but ready to go. Amy saw us sitting on the back steps and asked, "Are you too tired to go see Dr. Dixon?"

"No, ma'am, just tired of working," I told her truthfully.

"Well then, it's time to take a break and leave the Center for awhile. I have two errands in town and thought that if you three could possibly get clean enough to get into my car, then we would go into town first, before heading over to see Dr. Dixon. What do you say?" Amy asked.

We each kept an extra change of clothes at the Center because we've been this dirty before. Actually, we've been dirtier. I remember that when Katie was first cleaning the animal pens, she would get so dirty and wet that she would look just like a mud pie. Really. I remember Amy having to hose her down one day. It was funny. Nobody would let her in the car or house until she cleaned up. She was covered in mud, straw, fur, and, probably animal poop. It's funny how people say they love you, but when you get real dirty, no one wants to be near you.

We changed our clothes and got the straw out of our hair. Katie and Christina even took time to comb their hair! I didn't. We climbed into Amy's Suburban, the biggest car that I have ever been in. Katie wanted the front seat. I didn't care – she could have it. The back seat, no, I mean the second seat because there is another one behind this one, is big. It's like sitting on your couch while you're riding in your car! I bet I could get five of my friends in the back seat and we could sit there without touching each other.

Amy's Suburban was stopped at the red light in Mountview. Then she turned right on to Main Street. There were cars in just about every parking place and people crowded both sides of the street. Mountview was a popular place these days.

We were finally able to find a parking spot. Amy pulled in and turned off the engine. "I need to go to Berry's Hardware Store and get a few things. But since we'll pass Bivens Candy Store on the way, we can stop in there first. Maybe we can get something for later, as a reward for cleaning those very dirty cages," Amy proposed.

"Yeah, I know just what I want," Katie said as she got out of the front seat. "I want M&M's!"

"I want jelly beans," Christina declared.

We walked by the windows of the Mountview Real Estate office. Mr. Bill Martin was sitting inside at one of the desks. Amy tapped on the glass as we walked by and offered a friendly wave. Mr. Martin looked up and waved back.

Amy was in the lead and I was walking next to her. The girls were behind us, still talking about candy. The day was sunny and warm, not too hot. The people who passed us on the sidewalk all seemed to be friendly - several even said hello. It's nice being in a town where people aren't afraid to say hello to each other.

We reached the courtyard and the third door on the right was my favorite store in Mountview. The door opened with the customary jingling of the bell. We walked inside and I stood for a moment just to breathe in the wonderful aroma. It was a different world inside Bivens Candy Store. There were several customers browsing through the huge candy displays. The colorful arrays presented endless options. A kid could stay here for days without making a decision because there were so many choices. The smell of all that candy was kind of confusing at first. But with time, I could sort through the aromas and pick out the rich smell of chocolate. When I closed my eyes, I could smell the sweet scent of strawberry. There also seemed to be a hint of cinnamon in the air and, yes of course, there was peppermint, too.

I was jolted out of my reverie when Amy, who was still standing next to me, said, "Good morning, Jim."

Mr. Bivens was filling one of his many candy barrels. He looked up and smiled. "Good morning, Amy, Austin, Katie, and Christina. Well, you seem to have the whole crew with you today."

"Hello Mr. Bivens," we replied in unison. He was standing in the jelly beans section. Christina ran to join him. "Wow, look at all the jelly beans!" she exclaimed. There were heaps of barrels filled with multi-colored jelly beans. Each color meant a different flavor. There had to be twenty different barrels, which meant twenty different flavors. Coming to Bivens Candy Store was like playing a real life version of Candy Land. I was looking for a slide.

Mr. Bivens noticed us looking at all the jelly beans. "They look pretty good, don't they? Hey, I've got something new today. The distributor has a new product and maybe you guys would like to try it. I know you're Turkish Taffy fans; we're testing a slightly different version that's from the same company," he informed us.

Mr. Bivens walked back behind his cash register and the main candy counter. He reached inside a box and brought out several packages of brightly packaged candy.

"These are Turkish Twists. It seems that they have the same creamy taffy as the taffy bars, but they are bite size. You can take one and put it into your mouth, like this." He unwrapped a piece of the candy and popped it into his mouth. "It's hard, so you can enjoy the juices for a long time. But the really cool thing is…" His voice trailed off for a moment as the candy softened in his mouth and began sticking to his teeth. "Like I shaid, thish taffy warms up in your moush; it changes from hard to shoft. Then you get to chew."

Katie and Christina were laughing.

Mr. Bivens had to stop talking and concentrate on not drooling. He added, "It lasts a long time and you still get a creamy, vanilla flavored taste. If you would like to try some of these, I'd be happy to give you a bag."

"I think that would be great," I said enthusiastically.

Amy grinned. "That was a convincing demonstration, Jim."

"It's one of the benefits of the job, Amy," Mr. Bivens smiled. He turned to the rest of us.
"Well here, kids, try some of these Turkish Taffy Twists and, next time you stop by, you can tell me what you think. I told the distributor that I would help get him some market feedback. And, you can be my market feedback. The best part is, they're on the house."

"Thank you, Mr. Bivens. These will be great. We'll let you know what we think," I promised as I reached in the bag and grabbed several pieces.

The girls did the same and also thanked Mr. Bivens.

"How about you, Amy, do you want to give me some market feedback?"

"Jim, I think that I'll do the reporting this time and let the children do the research," Amy demurred.

"Suit yourself. Always good to see you, Amy. Tell Steve to come by. I haven't talked to him in the longest time," Mr. Bivens said as he watched us walk out the door.

"I'll do that, and thanks," Amy replied.

We all thanked Mr. Bivens one more time as we walked out of the store.

You could hear the crinkling of candy wrappers as we each crammed a Turkish Twist into our mouths. We were slobbering and drooling before we even got to the main walk.
As we headed west, we had to walk single file due to the number of people coming towards us.

"Wow, they must be having a sale at Berry's," Amy said jokingly.

Since our mouths were practically glued shut from the taffy, all we could do was nod our heads in agreement.

I don't believe that I have ever seen this many people in Mountview. We approached Berry's Hardware Store. We walked by the shovel display and a wheelbarrow with a sign indicating they were having some kind of sale. Next, there was a row of pots with some kind of flowers in them, in a neat and orderly display in front of the store. We finally made our way to the front door, which was open.

"Good morning, Mrs. Berry," Amy said.

"Good morning," Mrs. Berry responded, her back to us. When she turned around, she saw that there were four of us.

"Harold! It's the Austin kid and his sister and friends!" Mrs. Berry called out, facing the back of the store.

Mrs. Berry's short conversations were just the opposite of her husband's. Harold Berry entered the store from one of the back rooms.

"Howdy, folks," he said as he approached.

"Hewoh, Mishter Barwe," three of us said, unable to unstuck that taffy from our teeth. We started to laugh. The taffy was great. I could see that Katie was definitely drooling.

Mr. Berry raised an eyebrow and smiled.

"They're trying out a new candy, that's all," Amy offered by way of explanation.

"Interesting. Well, what can we do for you today, Amy?" Mr. Berry inquired.

"Mr. Berry, I need two rolls of duct tape, some fluid for my Coleman lantern, and a twelve-inch blade for my hacksaw. Can you help me?"

"I'll get the lantern fuel for you and the tape is right over there." Mr. Berry pointed to a tape display on the far side of the store. "Just pick out what you need and, Margaret, would you give Amy one of the twelve-inch hacksaw blades right where you are?"

I was looking at some cool stuff in an aisle that had a bunch of animal traps. I chewed and swallowed my first piece of taffy. It was great – exactly what Mr. Bivens told us it would be. I didn't know where the girls went, but then I heard some giggling coming from the paint department. I don't know what's funny about paint, but then again, I don't know girls.

I looked up and saw Amy at the cash register paying for her items, so I went over to join her.

"Thanks, Mr. Berry," Amy said. Then she looked up in an attempt to locate Mrs. Berry who was somewhere at the back of the store. She called out, "And thank you, Mrs. Berry!"

Amy turned back to Mr. Berry. "I always appreciate being able to ask you for something and you taking the time to find it, instead of me spending time trying to find it by myself. This is great service, Mr. Berry."

Mr. Berry responded as if on cue with a quote, "'He who asks may be a fool for five minutes. He who doesn't is a fool for a lifetime.' That's a Chinese proverb."

Amy stood there and looked at Mr. Berry for a moment without saying a word. Then she said, "Mr. Berry, it just amazes me that you have a quote for just about anything and at any time. You must have a very quick mind, sir."

It was obvious that Mr. Berry was pleased with that remark because he smiled. "Amy, you are so kind - thank you. Some people think that I don't have an original thought in my head. But I do. I just feel that if someone said something that was profound enough to be remembered, then why should I try to say something different? I will just use their words. Don't you think that makes some sense? Why should I try to perfect perfection?"

"Well said, sir. I don't know why you should - especially when you have a mind that can remember all those quotes. You have a gift there, Mr. Berry," Amy said earnestly.

"We all have gifts, Amy. Some of us use them, some of us don't. As far as you, Amy Bryant, remember this: 'A little fragrance always clings to the hand that gives you roses.' And your hand is always giving roses, Amy. Thanks for the kind words."

"You're welcome." Amy looked around the store and said, "Come on, kids, one more stop before we go see Dr. Dixon. Let's go."

The three of us followed behind Amy, calling goodbye to Mr. and Mrs. Berry.

"Remember," Mr. Berry began, as we walked out the door, "'The words that enlighten the soul are more precious than jewels,' according to Khan."

And then we heard Mrs. Berry bellow, "Harold! Enough is enough!"

There was a new store in town called Jake's Outfitters, and we wanted to see it. The store was located about a block from Berry's. It was a nice looking building - the red brick looked new, and the front windows were large and filled with cool things that we all enjoyed looking at. There were racks of clothes up and down the aisles, a hat section, and, over near the back, I could see some kind of boats. They looked like the one that Dr. Dixon had in his truck. We didn't have a lot of time, but since we were already there, we wanted to take a look. I immediately went over to inspect the boats, life jackets, fishing stuff, and several other things that looked interesting.

"Hey, there's a boat that looks like Dr. Dixon's," I commented.

There were several kayaks on display. A green kayak with black stripes was hanging from the ceiling and a red one, just like Dr. Dixon's, was on the floor. I went over to the red one and looked inside. I heard someone say, "Hey, Austin, how are you doing?"

I looked up to see Billy Johnson, our local reporter.

"Hey, Billy!" I replied.

"Are you thinking about getting a kayak?" Billy asked. "I hear that they're really fun."

"Oh, no. At least not yet. I saw one just like this today - it was Dr. Dixon's," I replied.

"Dr. Dixon has a kayak? Wow, that guy sure lives life to the fullest," Billy said admiringly. A boy about my age, who was like a younger version of Billy, approached us, grinning "Hey, Austin, I want you to meet my kid brother, TD. TD, this is Austin - he's the guy in that story I covered last month."

TD nodded. "Hey, Austin."

"Hey, TD." I nodded back, trying to seem as cool as he did.

"Yeah, TD and my mom and dad are up here for a little while to see what life is like in Mountview. My story, you know Austin - your story - got some play back in Atlanta and my family wanted to see where it took place. In fact, my mom and dad are over there." Billy pointed towards the camping section. "Let me get them. They'll want to meet you. Hey, looks like TD and you are about the same age." He walked away to find his parents.

TD was looking at the boat. I looked at the boat. There was an awkward silence.

Finally he said, "TD is *not* really my name. It's Logan."

"Then I'll just call you Logan," I said. "Austin really isn't my first name either. My first name is Bob. But I don't like it. Call me Austin." I waited a moment and asked, "So, how did you get the name TD?"

Logan said, "I'll tell you if you tell me how you got the name Austin."

I liked this guy already.

"OK, you first," I said.

"Well, my real name is Thaddeus Logan Johnson. Do I need to say anything more? I tried Thad, Ted, but nothing worked. Then I tried TD. If I *was* a ball player, like my brother, it would work. But I'm not. You know, TD as in touchdown? Well, it just isn't me. As much as my brother would like to have me be a football star like him, it just isn't going to happen. He calls me TD all the time. I wish he didn't."

I looked behind me to make sure his brother wasn't on his way back. "So, he still calls you TD?"

"Yep! But I want to be called Logan. OK, now it's your turn, **Bob**," Logan grinned.

"OK, TD, I'll tell you. Bob, Bobby, Rob, Robert – I've tried them all. None of them work. So I use my middle name too - Austin." I paused for a moment. Then I held my hand up. "So, what do you say, **Thaddeus**, is it a deal? No more first names, only middle names?" I asked, using Thaddeus to get back at him.

Logan and I high-fived, to seal the deal.

Right at that moment, Logan's family showed up. They must have been wondering what we were up to.

"Well, look here," Billy smiled, "I told you folks that this town is full of surprises. We have TD and Austin becoming fast friends. This is a record for my man TD."

Mr. and Mrs. Johnson were very surprised as they looked at us. Apparently, Logan didn't make friends that easily. But, to me, Logan was funny and honest and we had the same problems with our names. I liked the guy.

That's how it started – that was the day Logan and I became the best of friends.

I thought that I would take that moment to make a point. So I said, "That's right, Billy, Logan and I have decided to bury the name TD. Maybe that piece of news can make the morning edition?"

Logan's parents started laughing. Logan smiled as he turned to look at Billy. He thumped me on my back.

Billy's startled expression changed to a smile of understanding. "OK, I got it. I got it. OK, the name TD is over. And hello, Logan."

Amy approached from behind me. I didn't realize she was there until she spoke. "Hello, Billy. Hey, Austin, who are your friends?"

"Hey, Amy," Billy said. "Amy, these are my parents - William and Janet Johnson. Mom, Dad, this is Amy Bryant and this is Austin Cook, the ones that I wrote the stories about."

"Well, Billy has spoken so highly about the both of you. We are so happy to meet you." Mrs. Johnson said. Mr. Johnson smiled at us.

Billy quickly added, "And, Amy, this is my brother." He paused for a moment and looked at Logan. "This is Logan."

Apparently, the name TD had ended and, perhaps with it, the realization that Logan was never going to be a football star.

Logan, I would later learn, had another gift - a gift that would prove to be invaluable to him, to his family, and to me.

We enjoyed our conversation. Billy was bragging about the story he had written, and then he bragged about Amy and me. The attention was nice. But Amy realized we were running late when she looked at her watch. "I have enjoyed this. But we must be going. We are really proud of the job Billy is doing here in Mountview. I'm sure you two are proud as well." She paused for a moment. "You know, since you are visiting, why don't you all come over for dinner tonight? Steve, Austin's uncle, is a great griller. We were planning on burgers tonight. Steve makes the world's best burgers."

"Oh, thanks, but on such short notice, that would be too much of an inconvenience," Mrs. Johnson protested. "But thank you so much for asking."

"We really have to be leaving." Amy looked at her watch. "But I won't leave until you agree to come over. Our restaurants here in Mountview are excellent, but nothing beats a great grilled burger. We're grilling out anyway. It's easy for me to stop by and pick up a little more ground beef. We already have everything else. Wouldn't you like to learn a little more about Mountview?"

"Hey, Mom, Dad, let's go have a burger with them," Logan pleaded.

Mr. Johnson said, "This is very nice of you. We would love to come. What time would you like us to be there?"

It was settled. The Johnsons would join us at six-thirty for dinner. Great!

As we walked out the front door I noticed a sign in the window. Curiosity got the better of me and I stopped to read it. It said:

> We are losing Earth's greatest biological treasures. Rainforests once covered fourteen percent of the earth's land surface - now they only cover six percent. Experts estimate that the last remaining rainforests could be gone in less than fifty years. Rainforests are being destroyed at the rate of 1 ½ acres per second! Shortsighted governments, multi-national logging companies, and landowners only see the value of the timber. But nearly half of the world's species of plants, animals and microorganisms will be destroyed or severely threatened over the next quarter century due to the loss of our rainforests. We are losing approximately one hundred plant, animal, and insect species every single day due to rainforest deforestation. That is about fifty thousand species a year. Write your Congressman. Save our Natural Resources -they might save you one day.

I had a feeling that this was the work of Dr. Dixon. I was looking forward to seeing him and we were already late.

Chapter 11

Mr. Smith and Mr. Jones began their ascent of the mountain pathways. It wasn't that difficult. They climbed and stumbled, and climbed and stumbled and eventually reached a ridge that ran above their hideout. But they wanted to reach the top of the mountain, and it looked like they had one more section to climb. Mr. Jones found a pathway, which led them between several towering rocks and up through one more, claustrophobic passage. They would not have made it without the aid of this pathway - it appeared to be the only way to the top. It was a tight fit, especially for the plump Mr. Smith.

"Are you having a hard time?" Mr. Jones asked. "You need to be very careful."

Mr. Smith appreciated his partner's concern.

Mr. Jones added, "If you push your stomach any harder, I'm afraid twenty or thirty of those Twinkies will come shooting out of you like torpedoes from a submarine."

"Leave my Twinkies out of this," Mr. Smith said, panting.

Mr. Jones laughed heartily.

They climbed up the narrow path, grabbing on to anything that would help them reach the summit.

Once they reached the top of the mountain, they were treated to an awesome vista - a beautiful field of vibrant golden plants, thriving within the shade of a protective grove of hardwood trees. The rippling sea of yellow reminded them of a large room with wall-to-wall golden carpet. A gentle breeze caused this sea of yellow to softly sway to the rhythm of the wind.

"Look at these yellow flowers," Mr. Smith pointed out. He was gasping, but between short breaths he added, "I ain't ever seen such pretty flowers. And look – raspberries!" He bent down to touch the bright red, glistening berries. "I haven't had a raspberry for a real long time." He then proceeded to pick some.

"Stop thinking of your stomach and do some reconning, will ya? Don't do that," Mr. Jones ordered, grabbing Mr. Smith's hand and forcing the berries to drop. "They don't look like raspberries."

"OK, OK. You don't have to hurt me," Mr. Smith protested, rubbing his hand.

Mr. Jones surveyed the mountaintop. "We need to walk around the edge and see if there is another trail." While he was speaking, he turned his back on Mr. Smith who proceeded to grab a bunch of the berries and shove a handful of them into his pocket.

"Come on. Let's see what's up here," Mr. Jones instructed. "You walk on that side over there, and I'll take a look on this side."

They went in different directions through the golden flowers nestled quietly on the remote mountaintop. Mr. Jones didn't find another way off the mountain, only the way they had gotten there. Mr. Smith didn't pay close attention to what he was supposed to be looking for. They walked around the entire area without finding another exit. They were soon back where they started.

"Well, I didn't see anything, did you?" Mr. Jones asked.

"No, not a thing," Mr. Smith answered quite honestly.

"Then there must not be another way to get off the top of this mountain, except the way we came," Mr. Jones said thoughtfully. "And that's good. No one will be coming up to us from this side. Let's go back."

The proof that this statement was not accurate was overlooked by Mr. Smith who should have been paying attention to his detail, as opposed to thinking of the berries. For, on the back side of the mountain, there was a trail that led down another pathway to an opening in the mountain.

That mistake by Mr. Smith would prove to be critical.

Mr. Smith and Mr. Jones weren't the only ones looking around the mountaintop at that moment. If Mr. Smith had been paying more attention, he might have noticed a pair of beady eyes glaring at him from the underbrush - from the exact area where Mr. Smith had just been. The eyes were fixed and steady - studying his every move. The owner of those eyes did not want to take any action just yet, but he was ready to make his move in a split second if necessary…

Mr. Smith and Mr. Jones wearily returned to the path, retracing their steps, satisfied that they were safe, basking in their own ignorance.

Mr. Smith wanted the berries very badly. He marveled at the bright yellow flowers and ran his hands through them as he walked behind Mr. Jones. *Oh, I want to taste raspberries once again,* he thought. He remembered how delectable they tasted when he last ate them, so many years ago. He plucked a berry off of a plant and examined it. Maybe Mr. Jones was right? They didn't look like the raspberries he ate when he was a child. But then again, he couldn't remember exactly what raspberries looked like anyway. So, what was the big deal? It wasn't like they would kill him or anything.

They nearly had reached the path entrance, which was also the only exit. Mr. Smith grabbed at a handful of berries from a nearby plant. He pulled very hard, and ended up with the entire plant, berries, and the root ball, all hanging loosely in his hand. He examined it as they walked. It was more than he wanted, but it was fine. He noticed that at the stalk, which had bent while he was pulling, there were a few drops of yellow sap, or liquid, which had oozed out and some of it got on his right index finger. He didn't like it. It had a strange smell. He sniffed his finger – it was a licorice smell. The smell was nice, but the yellow stuff was very sticky. So he wiped it off on his pants, which left a bright yellow stain on the front, between his pocket and his zipper. Walking with the plant made him look as if he was carrying a parasol with red berries dangling from the top. Mr. Smith moved it up and around his head, blocking the sun, playing as if it really was a parasol.

Mr. Jones, anxious to climb down the mountain, reached the pathway that led back down to their hiding place and stopped. He turned around and noticed the plant that Mr. Smith was holding. "What are you doing?"

"I'm taking some berries back for breakfast," Mr. Smith replied, always thinking of his stomach.

"Oh, why do I put up with you?" Mr. Jones wondered out loud, shaking his head. But what could he do?

Mr. Jones started down the path, wanting to hurry back to their hideout. Mr. Smith, and his plant, followed close behind. They inched down, slid a bit, then they walked on the path that was more level. Then they slid some more, kicking up dust. Soon, rocks began to slide. The path seemed trickier going down the mountain than it was coming up. Mr. Jones slid, but caught his balance. Mr. Smith slid and stumbled some more going down through the treacherous pass. Here, it was narrow and a tight fit for both of them and especially tight for the overweight Mr. Smith and his berry branch.

Mr. Jones reached a wide opening. Small stones made this section exceptionally slippery. He held onto a rock, but his feet slid. He regained control and inched down the path.

Mr. Smith eventually reached the wider area that Mr. Jones had just traversed. Mr. Smith wasn't as fortunate. He slipped and lost his footing; it was only a matter of time. He regained his footing only to lose it again on a patch of dangerously loose rocks and stone. His feet were shooting rapidly down the pathway; gravity was taking over, pushing him faster and faster. He grabbed frantically for something to hold on to, but luck was not with him.

"Whoa, whoa!" he screamed. "Look out!" He was totally out of control.

Mr. Jones turned to see what the problem was. At that moment, Mr. Smith slammed into his partner, knocking him to the ground.

Boom!

Thud!

They were now both skidding down the rocky terrain, screaming at the top of their lungs, totally at the mercy of the mountain. Mr. Smith cried like a baby as he slid down the hill, the rocks tearing at his clothes and scraping his exposed arms. Berries flew off the branch, scattering along the path.

Both men were desperately reaching out, trying to grab onto anything that would slow their pell-mell descent. They clutched at the branches of bushes, but the branches broke. They reached out to grasp onto the large rocks that they were tumbling over, but their hands just slid off. They grabbed each other, but to no avail.

Finally, Mr. Jones, who was still out in front, reached out and held onto a bush that slowed his descent. His hold on the bush, in turn, slowed the tumbling Mr. Smith.

He held on tightly as the rocks fell and slid around them. Mr. Jones held on. The rocks stopped rolling, the dust began to settle, and the two men began to think they were safe. They were both lying on the ground and simultaneously took a deep breath, relieved that their ordeal was over.

However, at that moment, the strain on the lone bush that Mr. Jones was hanging onto like a life preserver began to give way.

Crack!

Crack!

SNAP!

Mr. Jones looked up, his eyes open wide with astonishment. He watched the bush uproot, and, although he still held on, the ground released its hold on the bush, causing both men to tumble through the air, headed toward the ledge below.

Thud!

Mr. Jones landed on top of a rock ledge, which stopped him from going any further. He looked up to see Mr. Smith flying towards him like a projectile. Mr. Smith landed on top of Mr. Jones, then he bounced and rolled over him. At the very last moment, Mr. Jones reached out and grabbed hold of Mr. Smith's shirt.

They had finally stopped.

Mr. Smith, realizing the ordeal was now over, slowly opened his eyes and, what he saw terrified him.

"Ahhhh!" he screamed.

Mr. Jones had stopped him at the very edge of the cliff. His arms were dangling over the ledge, and he was looking out into open air, down at the vast canyon below him. One more foot and Mr. Smith would have gone over. That was way too close for comfort. They both looked over the ledge and marveled at their luck.

Mr. Smith trembled uncontrollably, aware of how close he had come to plummeting over the edge of the cliff. His mouth was open, his breath was short and he watched as the berry-laden yellow plant plummeted the mind-numbing distance to the bottom of the canyon floor. The two men looked at each other and, without saying a word, knew how close they had come to having their lives come to a smashing end.

Neither man moved. Mr. Jones finally managed to take a deep breath. "If you ever do that again, the next time I won't stop you."

Mr. Smith replied, "I bet you would."

Mr. Smith cautiously eased away from the edge. He rolled over and came face to face with Mr. Jones. Both men were still laying on the rock, counting their blessings.

"If you would have let me fall, then you would have my blood on your hands for the rest of your life!" Mr. Smith muttered.

Mr. Jones countered, "I wouldn't have your blood on my hands...I probably would have cream filling and red raspberries there instead." He backed away from the edge to give himself some room, and noticed Mr. Smith's pants. "And what is that yellow stain there? Did you pee in your pants, too?"

Mr. Smith looked down at the yellow stain, "No! That was from that stupid plant. It wasn't me." He looked up at Mr. Jones to say something but the sun was shining in his eyes. He winced and covered his eyes. "Ooh! I would say something but the sun just blinded me."

Mr. Jones looked at Mr. Smith, then up at the sky. He sat up and pointed to the sun. "How can the sun be in your eyes when it's behind you?" He slowly turned around to find the source of whatever was shining in Mr. Smith's eyes. He looked up the mountain, where they had taken their fall, and noticed something gleaming brightly in the sun. "What the heck?"

Mr. Smith asked, "What is that? It's coming from the side of the mountain."

There was definitely something shiny, glistening in the sun - something that they hadn't noticed before - something that hadn't been noticed for hundreds of years.

Two hundred years, to be exact.

* * * * *

We hustled over to Dr. Dixon's house and ran up the steps to his front door. I was the first to get to the porch. The large knocker on the door has always fascinated me. It was brass and shaped like a lion's head – one day I expected it to open its mouth and roar! I reached out to touch it just as the door opened. I jerked my hand back in surprise.

"Well, look who we have here, some of my favorite people," Mrs. Dixon said warmly. Apparently, she had seen us running down the street. Or, maybe we were so late she was just waiting by the door. Whichever was the reason, it didn't matter. Mrs. Dixon was one of the nicest people that I knew. She could make me feel welcome any time. She is so nice I bet she would have let Katie, Christina, and me come over, even if we hadn't changed our work clothes.

Dr. Dixon came downstairs and greeted us as if we were his long lost family. "It's great to see you again."

I was thinking that I had just seen him that morning. But that was the way Dr. Dixon treated us. He was always really nice, just like his wife.

We talked about meeting Billy and his family, then we talked about Mr. Berry. Amy told Dr. Dixon that we saw his sign in the Outfitters window.

Dr. Dixon said he didn't write that piece. Rather, he saw an article that someone else had written and thought it summed up the problem quite nicely. "So I retyped it and hung it on the board at the Outfitters.

Someone might get angry that I didn't give them credit, but I just don't remember who wrote it, or I would have," he confessed.

Dr. Dixon had some papers for us to see and asked us to accompany him to his office. Mrs. Dixon asked Katie and Christina if they wanted to help her in the kitchen and finish baking the cookies. They quickly accepted. We would get some cookies later - if Katie and Christina didn't eat them all first.

"Now, where were we? Oh yes, you wanted to know about rainforests," Dr. Dixon said.

"Actually, sir, I wanted to know about plants helping cure people and animals," I corrected him.

"Oh yes, that's quite right. But you know I have so much information about rainforests; just look at this stack." He pointed to one of two piles of paper on his desk. "I thought that we could read through all of this together. That would be a great way to spend the day, don't you think?"

"It probably would, sir, but in order to read through that stack, we would be here for a lot longer than a day," I said uneasily.

"Of course - I was just kidding. However, there is some information that I thought you would like to know." Dr. Dixon picked up a book and flipped to his bookmark. "Ah yes, here it is. Norman Myers, in his book, *The Primary Source*, writes:

> Over one hundred prescription drugs currently sold worldwide come from plant-derived sources with a large number from rainforest ingredients. The U.S. National Cancer Institute has identified two thousand plants that are active against cancer cells with over fifty percent of these plants are found in the rainforest. Ninety percent of the rainforest plants used by Amazonian Indians as medicines have not been examined by modern science. Of the few rainforest plant species that have been studied by modern medicine, treatments have been found for childhood leukemia, breast cancer, high blood pressure, asthma, and scores of other illnesses.

Dr. Dixon continued. "In one of the articles in this stack, they say that specifically, Vincristine, extracted from the rainforest plant, periwinkle, is one of the world's most powerful anticancer drugs. It has dramatically increased the survival rate for acute childhood leukemia since its discovery."

"So, are there people out there looking for those plants and cures, now?" I asked.

"You read the article that I posted at the Outfitter," Dr. Dixon said. "As the rainforest species disappear, so do many possible cures for life-threatening diseases. I'm tempted to post it on every door in Asheville."

"Dr. Dixon, you have supported many causes since I've known you. But you are really fired up over this one," Amy remarked.

"So, we have cures for diseases but we're killing off the plants before we have a chance to find the cures?" I asked. "That sounds crazy." I looked at Amy who was nodding in agreement.

"Yes, in a word, yes. We may run out of time, too. The cure for so many diseases is within our reach. But we will run out of time. The pharmaceutical companies are helping us fight for rainforest preservation. They know that a cancer cure is growing out there in the rainforests, just waiting for us to find it. Wouldn't it be tragic for the world to lose the plant and lose the cure; a cure that would save millions of lives and relieve unimaginable pain and suffering. We have a chance to stop that from happening." He paused to let that sink in. "And yes, Amy, I *am* very fired up over this." He paused again and I could see he was beginning to get emotional. "See, we lost our niece to cancer. It is a very sensitive subject to me."

"Oh, I'm so sorry to hear that, Dr. Dixon," Amy said sympathetically.

"I'm sorry, too, Dr. Dixon," I said.

"Yes, it was tragic. And that adds energy to my fight. We need to save our rainforests," Dr. Dixon stated, changing the direction of the conversation.

"Is the Amazon the only rainforest in trouble or are there others?" Amy wondered.

"Do we have a rainforest around here?" I asked.

"Good questions. To answer yours first, Amy, yes, but the other rainforests are much smaller. There is one on the island of Borneo, another in Africa, and yes, we have one right here. Spirit Haven rests at the base of Mt. Pisgah, the fifth highest mountain in this region. Mt. Pisgah contains the first national forest of our nation and is said to be the guardian of healing plants in the area. The climate is temperate rainforest and each season brings distinct beauty. Asheville has the highest rainforest in North America. Did you know that the Appalachian Mountains, where Asheville is located, were once taller than the Alps?"

"Yes," I said. "I was just reading about that. Why aren't they still taller than the Alps?"

"The Appalachian Mountains have been around a lot longer than most mountain ranges. They are old and, after two hundred million years, they have become worn down due to weather. The Alps are young, just like the Rocky Mountains, but they will start to shrink, too. Just come back and measure them in two hundred million years," Dr. Dixon said.

"OK, I'll look forward to that. By the way, how do we know what kind of plants to look for?" I asked. "If I don't feel well, is there a book that tells me what kind of plant to eat?"

"Well, yes, there are books like that," Dr. Dixon responded. "However, with modern medicines and medical doctors, we usually go find a pill rather than boil a plant root. There are many folklore stories about plant cures - some real, but some are not so real. It's very important to be able to tell the difference."

Chapter 12

Mr. Smith and Mr. Jones were stunned - perhaps from the fall, perhaps from their unwitting discovery. They still didn't know what they were looking at, but the brilliant beacon was enticing them to investigate further. They got to their feet and peered through several rocks to gain a better view of their mysterious find.

They started to pull rocks away from the object. They pulled one rock away, then another, then another. The shiny golden object mesmerized them. They removed rocks faster and faster and faster. Now they could see it…or at least more of it. They were clawing at the side of the mountain. They continued removing rocks, at least the ones they could move, but the biggest ones were in the way. Mr. Smith reached over and attempted to dislodge an enormous rock. He grunted and groaned and the rock finally budged. Suddenly, the rocks above them moved, then the remaining rocks surrounding them began to shift. "Hold it!" he shouted. "Look! The whole side of the mountain is going to come crashing down!"

Mr. Jones stopped and peered inside the opening they had exposed which looked as if it led to a cave. The object slowly revealed itself with every rock they removed. It began to take the form of a statue, nearly four feet high with the appearance of some sort of animal. It was scarred and scraped and it was missing a big chunk of its base, but it was real. And it looked extremely heavy.

Now what were they going to do?

"If we move that rock," Mr. Smith began, pointing to the large rock positioned to the right of the statue, "all those rocks up there will come falling down on us. And we don't want that to happen, do we?"

Mr. Jones yanked his hand away from the rock. He was thinking about how to get to that object. Mr. Smith was right - if he moved the big rock that was situated right next to the statue, all the rocks on that side would come tumbling down on top of them. However, if they were able to move the rocks to the left of the statue, it wouldn't cause a rockslide since that side seemed to be more stable.

He decided that their best course of action would be to move the other rocks. But those rocks looked very heavy, and he wasn't sure that he and Mr. Smith would be able to move them on their own. He looked around to make sure that no one else was around. He wondered why they hadn't noticed it before. Apparently, the sun had hit the statue just right and that was what had given it away. The sun had come out at exactly the right moment. It had rained a little each day they had been there. He looked up and noticed that the clouds were gathering again. He knew how lucky they had been. For them to be at that exact location, at the exact time that the sun chose to peek out between the clouds…why…this had to be fate.

"This has to be fate!" Mr. Jones declared.

It was going to rain again soon. He didn't want to be up on the mountain, trying to get down to their hideout through that narrow and slippery path while it was raining. "Let's put a few of these rocks back and put some of those bushes on top to cover it up. Then we'll go back to our hideout before it rains again. The sun will be behind the clouds for a while and no one will see this hole. Then we can figure out what to do next."

But before they completely covered it up, Mr. Smith found a sharp rock. He struck the golden statue at a weak point and knocked a small sample of the golden idol into his hand. He put the gold piece into his pocket. "I don't want to go away empty handed," he explained to an inquisitive Mr. Jones. It just so happened that the gold landed in the same pocket as the berries.

The two men replaced several rocks, enough to cover up most of the statue. They placed several bushes back on top of the rocks. Satisfied with their work, they headed back to their hideout.

They continued their descent through the narrow pathway. Mr. Jones looked up when a few raindrops fell onto his face, causing him to squint. They moved faster and finally reached the path that would lead them back to their hideout.

The rain intensified. Soon, both men were completely drenched. When they got back to the safety of their hideout, their excitement overtook them. They talked about what they had just seen. They talked about the gold and what they were going to buy with the money. While they were talking, they started another fire in order to warm up and to dry their wet clothes.

Mr. Smith needed some kindling - something with which to start the fire. So he took the newspaper, wadded it up into several balls, and placed the pieces on top of where the fire had been earlier that morning. The coals were still hot and the paper quickly started to burn. "I hate to be burning the story about the movie studio looking for a movie site. We could be in the movies."

Mr. Jones shook his head. "When we get that gold, you won't need the movies; you can buy your own movie studio."

They both laughed.

The fire quickly consumed all of the paper, and Mr. Smith was now looking for something else to burn. There was a limited amount of kindling left and he put it all on the fire. The fire came to life and began burning brightly. As he fed the fire, Mr. Smith said, "I plan to buy a big house and have servants doing this."

"Make that fire bigger this time - we both need to get warm," Mr. Jones instructed.

They soon ran out of dry kindling, so Mr. Smith grabbed the only remaining firewood, which was left over from the night before and still wet. He placed the large sticks and smaller logs into the fire. Due to the dampness of the logs, the fire now began to produce a great deal of smoke, which rapidly filled the cave.

"What are you doing?" Mr. Jones asked, suddenly aware of all the smoke coming from the fire.

"I'm cold. I wanted to get the fire going," Mr. Smith explained. "We don't have any more dry wood."

"You're going to put the fire out that way. Get away and let me take care of it," Mr. Jones demanded, moving towards the fire.

The smoke from the wet wood not only blanketed the cave, but it poured out of the entrance as well. Apparently, this cave also had a rear entrance, and a draft was forcing the smoke outside. Mr. Smith noticed this. "See, we're all right. The smoke is going outside."

Mr. Jones got the fire going again using old Twinkie wrappers, cartons, and bags that they had taken when they had robbed the store. The flames were now rising high, and their welcome heat filled the cave as the thick, black smoke subsided.

"How did you do that?" Mr. Smith wondered, pointing to the fire.

"Don't worry about it – I'll take care of the fire," Mr. Jones commanded. He suddenly noticed Mr. Smith's right hand. "What's wrong with your finger?"

The index finger on Mr. Smith's right hand was rapidly ballooning and turning an alarmingly angry shade of red.

"I don't know," Mr. Smith said, holding it up to the light from the fire. "I must have jammed it when I fell." He examined it a little longer, then decided to change out of his wet clothing.

The warmth of the fire felt good. Mr. Jones put on more comfortable, dry clothes that he had stolen from the store. He now sported a sweatshirt and pants. Although the pants were way too short, they were dry, and he didn't really care what he looked like.

Mr. Smith, on the other hand, donned a pink sweatshirt that said 'Dixie Chicks' across the front, and a pair of red sweatpants that were way too tight. It was an interesting combination, to say the least!

While Mr. Jones heated another can of Vienna Sausages, Mr. Smith stuffed yet another Twinkie into his mouth. He didn't particularly like the pink Dixie Chick sweatshirt, but it was a lot more comfortable than his own soggy clothes. Mr. Smith had placed his wet shirt on a tree branch and was holding it over the fire, hoping to speed up the drying process. While he sat in front of the fire with the tree branch in one hand, he was attempting to gobble up the cream from inside the Twinkie in his other hand. If he had known that they were about to have company, he might have chosen a different outfit.

The sight of Mr. Smith adorned in his pink and red ensemble was the first thing that Calvin saw when he made his entrance into the cave.

* * * * *

"Folklore isn't true, is it?" I inquired.

"Folklore is full of truth. However, whenever information is passed down from generation to generation, some things are left out and ultimately forgotten," Dr. Dixon explained. He took off his glasses and began to clean them. "For example, onions fried in grease and put in cheesecloth make what mountain people called a 'poultice.' This was used to draw the poison out of an infected sore. Some used this on their dogs when the dogs were bit by snakes. I've heard that the cheesecloth would turn green after it was used for this purpose. Now, that is very possibly a real remedy, although I have never seen it applied. Also, the mountain people say that you should take onions and fry them in grease and then spread them on the chest of a sick person. After you do that, then wrap the sick person in quilts, and that will break a fever."

"How would you know? Boy that would stink so much that no one would be around to see if the guy got better," I joked lamely.

"It's very similar to the 'Legend of El Gato Dorado Grande,'" Dr. Dixon continued, putting his well-cleaned glasses back on. "It's a fact that gold was mined in this area. It is a fact that the Spanish explorers were claiming land in the sixteen hundreds and looking for that gold. It is a fact that one hundred years ago, many mountain lions roamed this area. It is possible that the Indians - I doubt that the Spanish would have - erected a tall statue of gold in the shape of a mountain lion to guard the entrance to their source of gold and, perhaps to honor the golden tawny cats that inhabited their land. So, in my estimation, the story and the facts have become a rather unsubstantiated legend, built on a pile of credible factual evidence. Legends and folklore all seem to have a basis in fact."

"Dr. Dixon, I have another question. Is 'The Curse of the Golden Gato' fact or isn't it?" I questioned.

"It is quite possible that the Golden Gato is for real, Austin. I have learned that it is better to spend my time dealing with facts, than dreaming of fiction. The facts clearly state that the possibility exists."

Dr. Dixon looked around and saw that we were all content with his answers. So he proceeded to his next question. "OK, now tell me about your trip to the Western North Carolina Nature Center in Asheville."

Amy began by giving Dr. Dixon a better understanding of Sarah's condition. Then I shared my experiences, taking time to describe Carrie the Cougar, Caruso, the big gray wolf, and, of course, the Eastern Hellbender. Dr. Dixon listened intently.

"Well, it sounds like you all had a very nice trip. I believe the Western North Carolina Nature Center is one of the biggest attractions in Asheville, and not only for nature lovers, but for people of any age who want to know more about the mysteries on our planet. I have always enjoyed my visits there," Dr. Dixon said warmly. "Now, let's discuss the most important issue, and that is Sarah's condition. How is she doing? When I was at the Center this morning, Sarah was still asleep, still recovering from her ordeal, I believe. I didn't want to wake her, but I want to know more about what happened."

We described Sarah's weak condition. I told Dr. Dixon about Sarah's ears beginning to change to rabbit ears. He was fascinated and wanted to know every detail. I described in more detail how her condition made her so weak that she couldn't remain in skunk form. However, once she ate the plant, she was fine.

"Now, tell me, what was the plant that Sarah ate?" he queried.

"I think Marcie said the name of the plant, but I was trying to hide at that time and didn't hear what she said," I admitted.

"I understand," he assured me. "If you can't remember the name, maybe you can remember what it looked like. Please describe the plant that you saw Sarah eating. You did say eating, didn't you?"

"Yes, sir, she was definitely eating the plant," I replied. "And, when I tried to get the plant away from her, she growled."

"Growled? Sarah growled at you?" Dr. Dixon asked in astonishment.

"Yes, sir, she growled big time. So I let her keep on doing what she was doing," I responded uneasily.

"Growled? Hmmm…" Dr. Dixon leaned back in his chair and looked at the ceiling. "OK, are there any details you *can* remember about the plant?"

"I'll try, but it was all over the floor when I got there," I reminded him.

"That's true." Dr. Dixon moved his chair closer to me as if he could get the information he was hoping for, just by looking at me. "So, Austin, how tall was the plant?"

"The plant was about this high," I said, indicating the height with my hands.

"What color was the dirt?" he asked.

"The color of the dirt?" I repeated. "What do you need the color of the dirt for?"

"That tells me where it grows. Was the soil red clay, sandy, or deep rich black?"

"I can't remember the color of the dirt," I admitted.

"Austin, please do your best to remember. Think back. Which of those colors do you think it was?"

"Uh, let me think. Dirt, color, floor, oh wait. I remember - the dirt was black." I paused for a moment and thought that I should say something funny. "And the pot that the dirt was in was clay-colored. Does that help?"

"We don't need a wise guy, do we, Austin? Your mind recorded these things. It's just that you didn't notice your mind recording these things. I'm just trying to get your mind to open up, that's all," Dr. Dixon said, raising his eyebrows.

"Yes, sir, I'm sorry." I closed my eyes. What did I remember seeing? "Wait. I remember the stalk of the plant was lying on the floor. I can't remember what it looked like." My eyes were still closed tightly, as I tried to make the picture become clear. "Wait, it was green. Yes, I remember seeing it now. It was green." I opened my eyes proudly.

"Good for you! I knew you had it in you. Now, how about the leaves of the plant? Did you see the leaves?" he prodded.

"The leaves were in Sarah's mouth. I can't remember seeing the leaves but I do remember seeing a couple of red berries. Wait, I do remember the leaves; they were dark, yellow leaves, maybe golden." I was remembering, after all.

"Good, good. This is very helpful." Dr. Dixon was writing my answers on a piece of paper on his desk. "OK, we are making real progress. Was there anything else that you noticed?"

"Not really, it happened so fast…wait, now this may seem to sound funny. But I remember thinking about licorice." I couldn't recall why. "I must have smelled licorice or something like licorice."

"Licorice? You were thinking about licorice? Isn't that interesting?" he mused.

"I was thinking about licorice because I smelled licorice. I bet it was on Sarah's breath," I said. That must have been it.

"OK, now we're getting somewhere." Dr. Dixon had written down my answers. He reviewed them. "Let's see, we have a plant about six inches high, in deep rich soil, with a green stalk, golden leaves, and red berries. You are doing very well. Do you think you can remember the name that Marcie called the plant now?"

"No, sir, but if I hear it again, I bet I would remember it," I said assuredly.

"OK, that sounds reasonable. Let's see here." Dr. Dixon turned his chair around in order to face some of the books in his office. There was a bookshelf behind his desk that ran along the entire wall from floor to ceiling. He got up and moved his finger along several book titles. He slowed down, then stopped. His finger tapped a book. "OK, I have got a book on this subject, right, oh let's see, yes, right here." He resumed his position in the chair and faced us. "Now, let's see what we can find out about this mystery plant that helps our Schmooney get healthy."

While he searched, I asked, "Are there a lot of Indian cures for diseases?"

"Oh yes," he replied as he thumbed through his book. He looked up for a moment. "American Indians used plants, trees and bark to keep them healthy. Did you know that willow tree bark is a natural aspirin? And the American Indians used black cohosh roots to make a tea to treat many conditions such as rheumatism, cramps, and epilepsy. It is also believed to hasten childbirth."

He returned to his book. He flipped through page after page, then continued. "Those are just a couple of examples. The Indians have a rich knowledge about natural cures. They passed a lot of that knowledge down to the settlers. The information is known as folklore. But treating sickness with plant cures can be tricky. Some of those plants look very similar. One plant can save a life, while another, very similar looking plant, can take a life." He stopped for a moment and looked at us to make an important point. "For example, the herb black cohosh should not be confused with the blue cohosh herb, which is used for different indications and has a greater potential for toxicity. You must be careful. Also, plants will affect an animal differently than they might affect a human." He resumed his search. "So, what Sarah was eating, which made her get better, might be fatal to you and me. Let me see, I am getting warm. Ah ha! OK here we go. Oh yes. I bet this is the one.

"Hydrastis Canadensis is a plant, native to Canada and the northeastern United States, and is found in the rich soil of shady woods and moist places at the edge of wooded lands. Did the plant that Sarah ate look like this one?" He turned the book around so that we could see the picture.

"It looks a lot like it. See the berries?" I pointed to the picture. "The leaves are golden. Yes, you found it."

"Let me read what it says. The goldenseal plant..." he read.

"Yes, sir!" I jumped up from my chair. "That's what she called it - goldenseal!"

"Very good, Austin," Dr. Dixon said. "It says here that goldenseal belongs to the buttercup family, though its leaves and fruit resemble those of the raspberry. It is a small perennial herb, six to twelve inches high, erect, cylindrical, hairy stalk with dark hairy leaves. The fruit is ripe in July and has much the appearance of a raspberry. Although the root, stalk, and leaves are beneficial for medicinal purposes, the red berries are not edible and, in quantity, can be poisonous to humans and animals. Early settlers learned of the virtues of goldenseal from the American Indians, who used the root as a medicine and its yellow juice as a dye for their clothing. When fresh, it has a narcotic odor, which is lost by age, when it acquires a peculiar sweetish smell, somewhat resembling licorice. The yellow color in the fresh root and the powder becomes a dark, yellowish-brown with age. When added to hot water, it produces a tonic, laxative alternative and detergent. It is a valuable remedy in the disordered conditions of the digestion. It has been used to treat hemorrhoids with excellent results. As a tonic, it is of extreme value in cases of habitual constipation."

"What does all that mean, Dr. Dixon?" Amy asked.

"Well, it means that Sarah ate a goldenseal plant - its leaves, its berries, and its root. Apparently, Sarah needed to cleanse her system, which she is doing as we speak, I suppose. She should be fine. She must have known what she was doing," Dr. Dixon mused. "Perhaps she smelled the licorice when you left her in her cage. She knew that the licorice-smelling plant was a cure and so she ate the plant."

"But the berries are poisonous to animals," I protested. "I remember that lady, Marcie, washing her hands when she found out about the plant. How did Sarah live through that?"

"Marcie knew that the toxicity could harm her. What that means is that if a human eats the berries, they would need to be near a bathroom due to the natural laxative in the plant. The yellow sap in the stalk would cause instant irritation and, if swallowed, the person could possibly die. If someone should drink a lot of the juice from the berries, well then," he chuckled, "they would probably need to live in a bathroom for a long period of time. That person would have violent stomach cramps and long periods of diarrhea resulting in a great deal of weakness.

"But with a Schmooney, her digestive track, metabolism, and, probably her whole body makeup, is much different than ours. She apparently found a cure a long time ago for a sickness that she contracted and she treated herself. She should be fine."

"It's like a vulture compared to a human. A vulture can eat diseased flesh and it won't hurt them," I commented, remembering Mr. Baker's discussion.

"You are exactly correct. Did you learn that at the Center?" Dr. Dixon asked.

"I learned a lot at the Center, yes, sir," I concurred.

"So it seems," Dr. Dixon said, nodding approvingly. "There is one more thing that you and I need to talk about, and that is improving your ability to send messages. What have you been able to do lately? Are you practicing the techniques that I have suggested?"

"Yes, sir, but I haven't had any luck. Matter of fact, I can't even send to Sarah. But that might be due to her being sick," I added.

"Well then, try and make this adjustment and see what happens. Keep trying to send to me, too. Let's use our imagery approach. That should work, but we won't get frustrated if it doesn't. Let's keep trying. Take a favorite picture of yours and think about it tonight. I will place a notepad by my bed and if I come up with an image, I will describe it, OK?" he asked.

"Yes, sir. I will." I hesitated. "I have one more thing to say. When I was at the Center, I met Leslie Ann who 'talks' to animals. She was pretty cool. She said that my gift might be bigger than we think. She also said that it might develop into something powerful. Do you agree with her?" I was looking at both Dr. Dixon and Amy.

Dr. Dixon took his glasses off again and sighed. The look he gave me was hard to read. Then he put his glasses back on and moved towards me. "Austin, your gift is very unique. It may develop into something very powerful and Leslie Ann may be correct. However, it may not. I want you to be prepared for either possibility, and that is why I stay so close to you. We need to approach this carefully and secretly. We do not want anyone outside of a few select people to know what you can do. There may come a day when you have to make some big decisions. I will help you prepare for that day."

"Don't be afraid of your gift, Austin," Amy interjected. "But always respect your gift. And respect the gifts that others have. We'll see how this all works out. I'm sure it will work out just fine."

I felt better. These were my friends and they would protect me. They both knew that I understood that.

Amy continued. "Dr. Dixon, I always learn so much when I'm here. You really have a gift for sharing knowledge. But now, we really need to get going. We have some guests coming to dinner tonight and Steve doesn't know it yet."

"Oh, Amy, then you'd better get going," Dr. Dixon agreed. At that moment, the door to his office swung open, and Mrs. Dixon, Katie, and Christina entered, carrying a white serving platter piled high with chocolate chip cookies.

"Ta-da!" Mrs. Dixon announced proudly.

We each had a delicious, fresh-baked cookie (I had two), and then we headed towards the Suburban to drive to the Center.

It was raining and, once again, we were getting drenched.

Chapter 13

The rain had been coming down for about fifteen minutes when Calvin realized they were in need of shelter.

Yes, they had brought a tent with them, and they were doing their best to pitch it, but pitching a tent on solid rock just wasn't going to work. They had been lucky yesterday. They had pitched their tent in a field with no problem, enabling them to stay dry. After their early morning hike halfway up the mountain, Calvin didn't want to try pitching the tent again if he didn't have to, and especially not on solid rock. He wanted a more substantial shelter and he definitely didn't want to get soaked.

So, Calvin decided it was time to find a cave…and find one fast.

He had heard that the cliffs had many caves, some better than others. He began by looking around from inside the canyon floor. He noticed how sheer the cliffs were. He also noticed several trails that headed up the sides. Whichever trail he chose, he and Woodrow would be better off not being loaded down by the tent.

He looked up around the rim, searching for a mountain with yellow flowers. From this vantage point, he couldn't find it.

He did see that there were different levels to the cliffs. He realized that in one direction they could climb all the way to the top without stopping; there wasn't a place to rest and it seemed to be straight up. It looked too formidable.

Then he noticed that to the east was a path with several ridges or landings. The ridges would give him and Woodrow a place they could rest. But more importantly, it would give him a better view of the mountaintops.

The best pathways seemed to be those that were carved through the rocks. Calvin walked over to get a better look. He could see that these paths were easier to climb. They were naturally cut into the sheer face in those areas that went straight up, but offered many handholds and footholds. It seemed that the sheer climbs were few and far between; there were mostly pathways where it would be possible for them to walk. His eyes followed one particular path up the mountain and he noticed several ridges. That would work for them.

Calvin remembered that there were many caves in the cliffs, and he presumed that the ridges would give him access to a cave. It was while he was studying this particular route that he noticed something unusual.

Smoke seemed to be billowing out of the mountainside. The rain was coming down a little harder now. Calvin wasn't sure whether he was imagining the smoke or not. So he looked harder. Sure enough, it was smoke. He told Woodrow to leave the tent. They were going to climb up to the point from which the smoke seemed to originate, about one hundred feet up the mountain. Woodrow, who was trying to secure the tent to some rocks, was relieved. He wadded up the tent and flung it onto the very rocks that were giving him such a hard time.

Goodbye and good riddance, he thought.

Calvin started out first and Woodrow followed, climbing through the narrow passages. Although they were going up, they weren't going straight up. The canyon floor was narrow at the base of the mountains, but the top was expansive. The cliffs were at about a sixty-degree angle. So there were short sections of the climb that went straight up, then there were pathways in between that were more like steep hills. While it was a difficult climb, it wasn't extremely taxing.

Calvin continued to look up, making certain that the smoke, or at least its source, was still in sight. The drizzle was making the rocks slippery, and that worried him. If he or his brother slipped, it would be a long, long drop.

He looked back and saw that Woodrow was keeping up with him. They were about to reach the first ridge, and he could still see the smoke. But the smoke seemed to blend into the rain, and it was becoming increasingly difficult to see.

They climbed faster.

Calvin made it to the ridge. He rested on one knee and studied the pathway as it wound east. Only a small amount of smoke was visible, but there definitely had to be a cave. And someone was there, all right. He wasn't worried. After all, he had his .357 Magnum right next to him.

Woodrow had now joined him. Calvin motioned to his brother to keep quiet and pointed to the cave, about fifty feet from them. Calvin took his gun out of its holster, making certain that it was loaded. It was. He put it back and snapped the holster guard over the gun, ensuring it wouldn't fall out.

They kept their gear on their backs and approached the source of the smoke. Calvin and his brother were very close to the opening. The smoke had disappeared. Calvin considered himself to be very fortunate to have seen the cave when he did. He reached down to touch his gun. It gave him all the confidence he needed.

"Let's go pay them a visit," he said to Woodrow, who was once again trailing behind him.

The rain was coming down harder now, concealing the sound of Calvin and Woodrow entering the cave. Calvin walked in first, followed by his brother. The packs on their backs dripped onto the floor of the cave. Their hats and their coats had water channeling off, and they, too, were dripping onto the cave floor. Calvin had his security, his .357 Magnum under his coat, ready to use if necessary.

"Hey, anyone in the cave?" he yelled, walking further into the cave.

That startled the unsuspecting Mr. Smith and Mr. Jones who looked up in surprise and simultaneously said, "Huh?"

Mr. Smith, tending to the drying of his pants, accidentally dropped them into the fire.

Both Mr. Smith and Mr. Jones stared in shock at the two brothers.

Calvin looked at them both with his wide, friendly grin. He noticed Mr. Smith's pants in the fire and remarked, "I don't know about you, but I like my pants medium rare."

Mr. Smith, with half a Twinkie hanging out of his mouth, snapped out of his stupor and retrieved his smoldering, wet pants, which had again created a plume of smoke.

Mr. Jones gulped down his Vienna sausage and said, "Come on in out of the rain."

"Thank you. Thank you kindly," said Calvin as he moved over by the fire. "It is really pouring out there. This fire is just what the doctor ordered." He took off his coat and hat and warmed his hands over the fire. Woodrow followed his brother's lead and sat down next to the fire.

Mr. Smith examined his smoldering pants while Mr. Jones rose, sizing up the Garner brothers.

Calvin looked directly at Mr. Smith, taking in his attire. "I see that you are a big country and western fan, are you?" He motioned to the pink Dixie Chicks sweatshirt.

Mr. Smith said, "Mmm," which was all he could muster with a Twinkie crammed into his mouth. Then he realized that Calvin was referring to the shirt that he had on. He finished chewing and said, "Oh yeah, kinda."

Calvin tried not to sneer. "Me, too. I'm a Johnny Cash fan, myself. But I don't usually wear any of his clothes."

Mr. Smith grimaced as he turned his pants on the stick.

Calvin continued. "We really appreciate you letting us come in out of the rain. It's right nasty out there. We haven't seen many people up here. We were real lucky to find this place, don't you think?"

"Real lucky," Mr. Jones agreed. He paused. "Are you boys passing through? Going fishing, hunting?"

"Oh, yeah," Calvin nodded as he warmed by the fire. "We're hunting and fishing guides and just taking some time off to check out this area. I heard that there are some real prizes up here in the Cliffs."

Mr. Jones said, "That's true. A lot of prizes - and a lot of surprises, too."

"You don't say. I was just telling Woodrow here…" he began, pointing to his brother. "Oh, wait. Where are my manners? I'm Calvin and this is my brother, Woodrow. I apologize for not introducing ourselves earlier." He offered his hand to Mr. Jones.

"I'm Mr. Jones and this is Mr. Smith," Mr. Jones said, shaking Calvin's hand warily.

"Oh, so we have Smith and Jones - how interesting. That should be easy for us to remember." Calvin paused. "So, what are you boys doing up here?"

There was silence. Neither Mr. Smith nor Mr. Jones had thought about what to say or how to answer that question since they had never actually expected anyone else to be up there. Finally, Mr. Smith spoke. "We're from a movie studio and we're scouting locations for a movie." He looked around to see everyone's reaction. But everyone, including Mr. Jones, just stared at him. He plunged ahead. "You might have read about us in the paper?"

Woodrow was impressed by this news. "I never met no movie studio people before. Tell me about the movies you've made."

Calvin, suspecting that this was a big fat lie, didn't let on. "Yes, I seem to have missed the news. Tell me what movies you've made."

Mr. Smith was stuck. He looked at Mr. Jones for assistance, but Mr. Jones was still staring at him, open-mouthed. "OK, sure," he said, just as he realized his pants were smoking again. He yanked them away from the fire and noticed a big, red stain on the front, which he examined closely.

Calvin repeated his question. "Uh, Mr. Smith, what *are* some of the movies that you've made?"

Mr. Smith looked up and exclaimed, "Look at my pants! They have this big red stain."

At which Woodrow rubbed his head and remarked, "I haven't seen that one yet."

Calvin looked at his brother in disgust. Mr. Smith, realizing that the red berries had caused the stain, placed his hand into his pocket to get the berries out. When he did, the chunk of gold that he had carved from the statue suddenly dropped onto the stone floor.

The sound of the gold hitting the floor wasn't that loud.

The impact of the gold hitting the floor was deafening.

Everyone saw it. Gleaming, shining, glistening from the fire's glow, the splendor of the golden remnant carved from the statue captured everyone's attention.

Mr. Smith froze in shock. Then he nervously looked around the room, aware that the three other men were staring hungrily at the gold. He cleared his throat. "Perhaps you've heard of 'Goldfinger?'"

Calvin knew this was his chance. He pulled his gun out of his pants, pointed it at Mr. Smith and said, "OK, Mr. Goldfinger, why don't you tell me, exactly where did you get that?"

Mr. Smith didn't say a word - nor did Mr. Jones.

"Woodrow, watch the big one over there," Calvin commanded, pointing at Mr. Jones. "I plan on talking to Mr. Smith one-on-one."

Mr. Smith stared at the gun. "Is that loaded?"

"Oh yes. But you don't have to take my word for it. Would you like to see a demonstration?" Calvin asked, without taking his eyes, or the gun, off of Mr. Smith.

"No, no need. I trust you," Mr. Smith replied nervously.

"Good. See, we're already getting somewhere. Since you trust me, then I should trust you. So tell me, Mr. Smith, or whatever your name is, where did you find the gold?" Calvin demanded, waving the gun at Mr. Smith.

"What gold?" Mr. Smith asked, attempting to sound innocent, as his pants fell into the fire, again.

Calvin cocked the gun, "I'm going to count to three. At that time, I'll prove to you that this gun is loaded. Your pretty little pink sweatshirt will have some rather serious red stains on it, just like those pants. Now tell me - where did you find the gold?"

"I can tell you," Mr. Jones said suddenly.

That got Calvin's attention. "You afraid that I'm going mess up your fat friend here?"

"Hey, there's no need for you to be so rude!" Mr. Smith retorted.

"I can tell you where the gold is, but first we make a deal," Mr. Jones offered.

"A deal, who said anything about a deal?" Calvin sneered. "I have the gun. I have the bullets. I make the rules. That is how the game is played, my friend."

"There's a lot of gold, and a lot of big rocks in front of it. It will take all four of us to get it out of there. You know people will be coming up here and snooping around. We don't have a lot of time to move it someplace safe." Mr. Jones waited to let that information sink in.

Calvin didn't say anything. Mr. Jones figured his talking was doing some good. He continued. "Half a gold treasure is better than none, don't you think? Telling you where it is won't keep us from getting shot, will it?"

"Well, you do have a point there," Calvin admitted reluctantly. "And you are exactly correct that half is better than none."

Calvin also knew that he didn't want to take a lot of time looking for the gold. The other two men already knew where it was. That was a good thing. Plus, he figured, he could always shoot them after they showed him where the gold was. "OK, we have a deal," he acquiesced.

"First, you give us the gun," Mr. Jones proposed. "We don't have a gun and who's to say you won't shoot us after we tell you where the gold is?"

Calvin realized that Mr. Jones was the smart one. But he shook his head. "I am *not* giving you my gun."

"Then you need to give me the bullets and you can keep the gun," Mr. Jones insisted.

"Now, let me get this straight…I have the gun and I have the bullets. And you want me to give you one of them. What makes you think I would do that?" Calvin asked.

"You don't know where the gold is, do you? You don't want to take a lot of time trying to find it, do you? And, two of you won't be able to move the big rocks. You need help getting all that gold, and there is a lot of it, out of there. And, why would you shoot two innocent people when you don't have to?" Mr. Jones added.

"The answer to your last question - I might just like shooting people. But, having said that, you do make some good points," Calvin conceded. He didn't really mind shooting them. He was mean and nasty and they didn't matter to him at all. But then again, there might be a better time for that later, after they found the gold and, after they moved the rocks. "OK, we have a deal. Here are the bullets." He emptied the gun.

"No, no. You might have more bullets. We'll hold the gun," Mr. Jones persisted..

Watch out for this one, he's smart, Calvin thought. "OK, we have a deal – here's the gun. Are you happy now?"

Mr. Jones accepted the gun and nodded his head.

"Good, we have that settled. Now tell me, boys, exactly where is the gold?" Calvin asked.

"It's not far from here. We can go when the rain stops, but it would be safest to wait until the path has had time to dry, probably tomorrow morning," Mr. Jones replied.

"Well then, it's settled. Let's get a good night's sleep so we can be ready for an exciting day tomorrow," Calvin said. He looked at Mr. Smith. "And, by the way, what's wrong with your finger?"

* * * * *

When we arrived at the Center, I immediately went to see Sarah. She was awake and sent me a message to come visit her in her room.

'So, how have you been?' I sent.

'I feel so much better. And I look like my old-self, too,' she answered.

She really was doing much better. Amy and Katie came into the room. Amy briefly checked on Sarah and suggested she stay put for the night. Amy arranged for Sarah to have some dinner, which consisted of lettuce, broccoli stems, and some dry food that was designed especially for skunks – they really did have something for everyone!

Christina's mom came by the Center and took her home. Then Amy called Uncle Steve and asked him to pick up more ground beef at the store since we would be having company for dinner. Uncle Steve was looking forward to meeting Billy's family and assured Amy that there would be plenty to eat. Amy told Uncle Steve that we would check in on Sarah one more time and then head home.

Sarah was lying on a blanket, with her head on one of her paws when she heard us approaching. She smiled at us sweetly, then she waved with her front paw. *'Come here, I need to tell you something.'*

Sarah thanked us for helping her and I relayed that to Amy.

Amy reached down and started stroking Sarah's back. "Tell Sarah that we love her and will do anything necessary to help her get well again."

I conveyed that message to Sarah while Amy continued petting her back.

Sarah sent, *'I know you all will always take care of me. And I will always take care of you. I love you all so much.'*

I passed that message on to the group.

Sarah placed her paw on my arm. *'I need to tell you a story. I will need your help again.'*

Sarah began. She told us about a time when she was very young and she was living here, in this forest, with her brother.

"You had a brother!" I shouted out loud.

Of course, this got Amy and Katie's attention.

'There are other Schmooneys?' I sent.

'Yes, Austin, there are other Schmooneys. It is time that you knew that.'

Sarah told me that a long, long time ago, she was very sick and her brother took her to a 'field of flowers' on top of a mountain in the middle of cliffs and caves. The mountaintop was carpeted with golden plants adorned with brilliant leaves and laden with red berries. The Indians knew the golden plant. They used the root of the plant as a medicine and its yellow juice as a dye for their clothing. Although the Indians used the root, they knew that the juice, the leaves and the berries were not edible. The leaves were considered poisonous, so the natives kept their children away from the plant. Since the plant was also considered poisonous to their livestock, they never transplanted the field. The berries, if consumed, would cause terrible cramps. But the strange thing was that what was poison to them was an antidote for a Schmooney. Schmoonies, just like humans, get sick from time to time. If the Schmoonies aren't treated quickly when they get very ill, just like humans, they might die.

I passed this information on to Amy and Katie.

Sarah told me that she would need to go get more medicine. She needed more plants to eat. Although she had received temporary relief from the one plant, it wasn't enough - her condition would return. She needed to find more plants very soon.

I explained this to Amy and Katie.

Amy nodded. "It's just like treating any sort of sickness or condition. When I prescribe antibiotics, I instruct all my patients to take *all* the medicine as prescribed. Even if the patient begins feeling better, they need to take every single pill. Sarah may feel temporary relief, and we may think that she has recovered, but we must kill *all* the bacteria in her system. The only way to accomplish that is having her take the proper amount of medicine. I understand what she is saying. Austin, ask Sarah where we can find more plants for her."

Before I passed that on to Sarah, I remembered my talk with Dr. Dixon. "Didn't Dr. Dixon say the only place the golden plant grew was in Canada and the northeastern United States?"

"Yes, I remember that's what he said. But that's a long way from here and we don't have time to go there." She thought for a moment. "So, where is this field of flowers? Is it still around here?"

I asked Sarah to tell me what she knew about the field of golden flowers.

'Yes, it is still there, as far as I know. It is a golden field found at the top of only one mountain in this area.'

She had never talked about having a family before. She told me that her older brother saved her. He had taken her to the field of flowers, where she had been able to get better. She told me it was still there.

I passed this information on. "We need to leave immediately before she gets any worse," I urged.

"Can Sarah get us back to the field?" Amy asked.

Sarah said she knew the general area and could get us there. But as far as which mountain, she had no idea. She advised me that she would be getting worse, quickly. She had enough energy at the moment. But if we were going, then we needed to leave the next day.

I relayed this information to Amy and Katie. "Maybe Dr. Dixon can help us. He knows this area."

"I'll call Dr. Dixon and ask him what he knows," Amy said. "Austin, we have a lot to do to get ready to go. Like figure out exactly where we're going. Maybe Steve will be able to give us an idea if Dr. Dixon can't help. Oh no, I forgot that we have company tonight for dinner!"

We told Sarah we would see her soon, then we headed to the house.

What a day it had been!

What we didn't know at the time was that the next day would hold even more excitement.

Chapter 14

When the Johnsons arrived, Uncle Steve had everything set up. It is amazing what can be done in a short period of time. The burgers were ready to be grilled, the grill was open for business and ready to go, we had plenty of Vernors Ginger Ale, Fritos, hamburger buns, and all the trimmings, as they say.

We changed again and this time we were showered and had on clothes that were actually clean. None of us smelled like the cages and animal pens anymore. Amy was prepared to be a gracious host, and even Edison and Franklin were on their best behavior.

After the traditional greetings, the big group broke up into smaller groups. I showed Logan the pictures in the den that Uncle Steve had taken. The big bear, the mountain lion - all the cool pictures. Katie and Amy told Mrs. Johnson about the local area, encouraging the Johnsons to move to Mountview. Uncle Steve, Mr. Johnson and Billy talked politics and sports. Uncle Steve was especially interested in Billy's career, brief as it was, in the major leagues.

Dinner was about to be served.

We were seated around the big round table, the one on the back deck, which had the large green umbrella. But since this was evening, the umbrella was closed and we could see an occasional star in the moonless night. Uncle Steve started talking about the area. Billy joined in, offering some interesting insight. I discovered that Billy had played football at the

University of Georgia and had always wanted his little brother, Logan, to follow in his footsteps. But Logan didn't play football. Logan was interested in writing.

We found out that Mr. Johnson was a history teacher and a coach for Laurens Middle School and the Johnson family lived in Laurens, South Carolina. Mrs. Johnson worked as a teller at large bank in the nearby town of Clinton. Mr. Johnson received his degree from Grambling State University and played football for Coach Robinson.

"You played for Eddie Robinson?" Uncle Steve asked.

"Yes, I did," replied Mr. Johnson.

"Who is that?" I asked.

"Coach Eddie Robinson is one of the legends of football," Uncle Steve explained. "He is one of the greats. He coached Grambling State University teams for over fifty years. He won more games than any other coach in football history."

"Wow!" I exclaimed. "So Coach Robinson is a football legend?"

Mr. Johnson nodded. "Coach's greatness wasn't only on the football field. He prepared his football players for real life. He knew that most of us would never play on Sunday, although two hundred of his players did. But since he cared so much for his school and his players, he made certain that we were ready to be players in the game of life after we left school. Every day, I appreciate what Coach has done for me."

"And you are a history teacher as well?" Amy asked.

"Yes, I am," Mr. Johnson replied. "I try to do the same thing and prepare my students for the real world. Yes, they are young in middle school, but students that age have to make big decisions. Those decisions are based on family conditions, the student's ability to stay in school, and, of course, peer pressure. So I try to prepare them for the next few years. Give them hope. Tell them the truth and keep them in school."

"They really need that kind of help," Uncle Steve remarked.

"Literacy is a big campaign for me. Many of our new students come to middle school and can't read at an acceptable level. No matter how much I work with the student, if the student can't keep up with the homework reading, then that student will fail the tests, and eventually drop out of school. I fail. My student fails. The whole system then fails," Mr. Johnson told us.

"You're right. The parents have to get involved, don't they? We can't expect the school system to do everything," Amy asserted.

"Did you know that South Carolina has the worst literacy rate in the United States? That's terrible, but the good news is that our state is doing something about it. I started a program in our school called 'Winners Are Readers.' The acronym is WAR and that is what we are declaring, war against illiteracy. WAR promotes the positive attributes of reading. Winners read. And if you want to be a winner, then read. If you are a reader, then you are a winner," Mr. Johnson said.

"So, how has the program done so far?" asked Uncle Steve.

"We're still in the early stages, but we are showing life and the Governor has endorsed the program. Actually, what is even better, the Governor's wife, our state's first lady, is on the board and that has given us a huge boost. We have several Title 1 schools showing great success," Mr. Johnson proudly informed us.

"Congratulations," Amy smiled.

"Well, the congratulations go to the State of South Carolina, the Governor and his wife, and the State House of Representatives who identified the problem and are doing something about it. Thanks go to those men and women." Mr. Johnson said modestly.

"Well, you don't hear about that very often," Uncle Steve observed.

Amy kept looking at her watch, wondering why Dr. Dixon hadn't returned her phone call.

"Mr. Johnson, since you know about legends, have you ever heard of the legend of the Golden Gato?" I wondered.

Everyone laughed.

Katie said, "Gato is Spanish for cat."

"Oh, is it?" asked Mrs. Johnson. "It is so good to have our children learning other languages."

"Yes, it is, and we are very proud of Katie," Amy said.

We all began to talk at the same time. Separate conversations took place that sounded like one of our classrooms when the teacher was out of the room.

"Yes, I have," I heard Mr. Johnson say.

The noise level was now calming down and silence replaced the chatter.

"Dad, yes, you have what?" Billy asked, looking around the table to see if anyone followed what his dad was talking about.

"Yes, I have," Mr. Johnson repeated and all of us looked at him blankly. He pointed to me. "Yes, I *have* heard of the legend of the Golden Gato."

"You have…really?" I asked enthusiastically.

"Yes. Well, I *am* a history major, remember? I try to keep my students aware of local historical events. It keeps their interest level up. I spend time in our library researching these stories."

"Where did you hear about the legend?" I asked.

"I don't think I heard about it. But I did read something about it," Mr. Johnson said. "I can't recall the details exactly, but something about Spanish gold in these mountains and there was a curse on it. Didn't it have something to do with a statue of a mountain lion that was made of pure gold? People would go to the mountains to see the golden statue and they would die or vanish - never be seen again, something like that."

"Yeah, that's it," Billy nodded. "I'm researching that for my paper. I didn't know you knew about the legend."

"Well, it pays to ask, doesn't it?" Mrs. Johnson smiled.

"Hey, Dad, I can use you as one of my unnamed sources," Billy joked.

"So, do you think it's for real?" I asked Mr. Johnson.

"Yes. Well, let me clarify – I'm sure parts of it are for real. That's the way legends go," he replied. "But it is always fun to think about it."

Amy was impressed with his knowledge. "Since you are such a source of information, do you happen to know anything about a field of golden flowers sitting high on top of a mountain, right around here? The golden flowers have bright red berries and, when the sun shines on them, they can be seen for miles and miles."

Mr. Johnson thought a moment and replied, "It sounds beautiful, but I can't say that I have."

"Oh, well that's too bad. It was worth a shot, don't you think, Austin?" Amy winked.

"Yes, I have," Uncle Steve murmured.

There was silence.

"Uncle Steve, yes, you have what?" I asked.

"Yes, I have heard of that field. It is in Waynesville Cliffs," Uncle Steve stated matter-of-factly.

"You have?" Amy asked in surprise. "How do you know about the field of golden flowers?"

"I was told by some of my friends who work for the state," Uncle Steve explained. "They saw it during one of their excursions for the State Wildlife Department to the mountains. It's not every day that you see a golden field on top of a mountain. They said it was quite beautiful."

"Did they go into the field?" I asked.

"No," Uncle Steve replied, "They didn't. They saw that the field was in Waynesville Cliffs, but they didn't actually go there."

"Do you know how to get there?" Amy asked, trying to contain her excitement.

"Yes, sure, it's not that difficult. But I have only been to the Cliffs once. It has a lot of tall peaks and it's dangerous. I could find Waynesville Cliffs without a problem. As far as finding that field, I could probably get you to the general area."

Amy made a mental note of this information, then directed the conversation to include the Johnsons. Soon, dinner was over and the Johnsons needed to get home, since they were going back to Laurens in the morning. We had an excellent evening. We were thrilled to have learned as much as we had, and we looked forward to our new friendship with the Johnsons. We all bid each other good night.

Uncle Steve was finishing his cup of coffee while sitting at the table. Amy was picking up the last few items from the table. Katie and I were helping her. "So, you know how to find your way to the Waynesville Cliffs?" Amy asked.

"Sure, I can find my way there," Uncle Steve responded.

"Well, that's good to know. Because we will be leaving tomorrow to go find it," Amy informed him.

"What?" Uncle Steve practically shouted, directing all of his attention to Amy.

"Do you want to go with us?" Amy asked. She proceeded to fill him in on my conversation with Sarah.

Uncle Steve hurried to retrieve maps of Waynesville Cliffs.

No time to waste.

We gathered around the table and planned our trip.

We quickly packed our gear. We took all the essentials: tents, sleeping bags, lanterns, dehydrated food left over from our last camping trip (plus we put some fresh food in the cooler), fire items, and I packed my personal survival gear. Uncle Steve took his rifle because he wanted to take every precaution – we weren't sure what we were going to find up in those mountains.

Our plan was to leave very early the next morning. We would drive to Prospect by 6 AM. Then we would go north to Hog's Head and, if we timed it correctly, we would hike into Waynesville Cliffs as the sun was coming up.

We finally went to bed. But none of us slept very well. Sarah desperately needed our help…and we knew there wasn't a moment to waste.

Chapter 15

We awoke to the new day. The sun wasn't up yet, but we were.

Amy and Uncle Steve had packed the Suburban the night before. All we needed to do was climb into the back seat and sleep.

Sarah was in her cage and the Suburban was loaded with our camping gear, food, water, tents, supplies, and everything else we could think of.

We backed out of the dark driveway and headed towards Prospect. Things had started well and we expected things to be going even better.

Katie and I were awake when we arrived at Hogs Head Park, which was the end of the roadway. We used the park's facilities and took time to drink water and eat some sandwiches that Amy had prepared for us. It was about ten o'clock in the morning.

Now came the hard part: we grabbed our backpacks, plus Amy carried Sarah, and Uncle Steve toted the additional equipment and his rifle. It would take us about four hours to reach our first destination, which also included time to rest along the way. We had hiked this distance before, so it wasn't anything new, except for caring for Sarah.

Amy had designed a sling-like pouch in order to carry Sarah. It was a sling similar to one I had to have when I broke my arm a long time ago. But instead of my arm, I could hold Sarah. It was additional weight, but she wasn't that heavy. We had agreed that Amy and I would share in the carrying of Sarah.

Uncle Steve and Amy had planned well. We arrived without incident at the floor of the canyon. It was just like Uncle Steve explained - a western canyon, with sheer walls that stretched up into the light. They don't really have canyons east of the Rocky Mountains. However, this was an exception. With the cliff's sheer walls and its flat floor, combined with no access into this area, many visitors called this a canyon.

We rested for a moment before we continued. I was excited. We were here to help Sarah and I was anxious to do it quickly.

* * * * *

Mr. Smith, Mr. Jones, Calvin and Woodrow were up before light. They were dressed and busy drinking coffee. They were waiting for the sun to come up in the canyon in order to have enough light to travel the pathways. Between the four of them, they had two shovels, one pickax, and several flashlights.

Although the sun was out, the thick cloud cover forced them to leave later than planned. The morning rays intermittently penetrated the rocky confines of the cliffs. The world of shadows came to life.

The four men left the hideout and headed towards the pathway that Calvin and Woodrow had ascended the day before. They walked the ridge in single file and, once they reached the pathway, they turned left and started to climb higher. The narrow passages presented the same challenges as they had the day before, but it took longer this time due to the additional tools they now carried. After an hour of slow ascent, they arrive at the gold mine ridge. Calvin figured that they had traveled another hundred feet higher. The dizzying view down to the canyon floor was a bit much, even for Calvin.

The men rested on the ridge. Calvin could see the top of the mountain at the next level, approximately fifty feet higher. But Mr. Jones didn't go in that direction. Instead, he turned east. "There it is," he motioned, walking to a spot on the side of the mountain. "We need to remove these dead bushes and some of the rocks and then you'll see it."

"This is about one hundred feet right above your hideout," Calvin observed as he cautiously peered over the edge. "It sure is a long way down."

"We almost fell over that edge yesterday," Mr. Smith announced.

"Boy, that was a lucky break for you two," Calvin remarked. What he was thinking was what a lucky break it was for him to have the gold so close by. He was marveling at his luck as he stared out over the canyon while the others began removing the smaller rocks and bushes from the entrance.

Calvin turned around and immediately noticed that there were several enormous boulders blocking the way. He watched Mr. Jones attempt to use the tools in order to dislodge the rocks. "If we can just get those big stones out of the way, we'll be able to get to it," he said. "I have some dynamite. We can blow those rocks away."

"Are you crazy?" Mr. Jones yelled. "If you use dynamite, you will bring the whole side of this mountain down on top of us."

"He's right," Woodrow agreed.

Calvin knew better. He just wanted to get out of there as fast as he could. He didn't like heights, but heights, falls, and accidents waiting to happen were all around him. "OK, if you're so smart, then what *should* we do? Does anybody have any ideas?"

"We can take these shovels and the pickax handle and put them in here," Mr. Jones suggested, pointing to a leverage area under one of the rocks to the left of the gold. "If we get the right leverage, then we can move this rock out of the way. There's nothing on top of it, so it shouldn't cave in on us." He looked at the other men and cautioned, "You don't want to move that rock on the right. If we do, all of that…" he pointed to the rocks above them, "…will come down on top of us. Come on, let's get going."

The four men labored to budge that one particularly stubborn boulder for several hours. The rock was firmly embedded, having rested in its place for many, many years, and it was unwilling to assist in its own eviction. The men tried prying, shoving, pressing, lifting, and even shoveling, but to no avail.

Mr. Smith was having a harder time than the rest of the men. His finger continued to swell, and it now throbbed painfully. The angry, red color had intensified, which Calvin suddenly noticed.

"What's wrong with your finger?" Calvin asked in disgust. "Why don't you wrap it up or something? It's making me sick."

Mr. Smith had been keeping an eye on his finger all morning. It itched and burned terribly and he was starting to worry about it. "I must have sprained it yesterday in the rock slide. I've never had anything like this before."

"You know, they say this gold is cursed," Woodrow remarked.

"Cursed?" repeated Mr. Smith.

Woodrow nodded.

"Cursed?" Calvin yelled. "And you think the curse is causing his finger to get red like a tomato and swollen like that? Not much of a curse, if you ask me."

Woodrow and Mr. Smith just looked at each other.

"The only cursing that's going to happen around here," Calvin continued, "is my language if we don't get these rocks out of the way. Now, let's get moving."

Woodrow focused on the rocks and rammed his shovel handle into the crevice. The other men did the same with their shovel handles, and slowly began to pry the rock from its resting place. Calvin supervised. Slowly, ever so slowly, the rock began to move.

"It's moving!" Calvin shouted excitedly.

They continued to apply pressure and, with the sure determination of the three men, the rock continued to shift. It moved a little...then a little bit more.

"Here it comes, boys!" Calvin exclaimed. "You're almost there!"

The boulder was slowly rocking back and forth. Suddenly, it flew out of its chamber and starting rolling towards the edge of the cliff.

"Look out!" Mr. Smith yelled.

Woodrow was caught standing between the rock and the edge of the cliff. He jumped out of the way as the rock barreled off the cliff and plummeted to the floor below, smashing into the sides of the canyon walls as it hurtled towards the ground.

BANG!

BANG!

BANG!

THUD!

The boulder finally came to rest on the canyon floor. The force of the dislodging of the enormous rock caused other rocks to fall along with it. It was like a meteor shower, raining down upon the canyon floor.

* * * * *

At first, we didn't know what we were hearing. Something was making a tremendous racket, but we had no idea what it was. Uncle Steve was in the lead, looking straight ahead. Amy was in the back, looking behind us. Katie and I were near the middle, and I was looking straight up.

That's when I saw it!

"Avalanche – look out!" I yelled at the top of my lungs. I grabbed Katie's arm, and the two of us followed Amy as she raced to the side of the mountain. There was a protective ridge about ten feet above the canyon floor. It provided the cover we desperately needed as a gigantic boulder smashed right in front of us. Then a storm of rocks and stones pelted the area.

We had reached a safe spot and were fine. But Uncle Steve had the farthest to run. He had avoided the huge boulder, but was stuck in the fallout. A massive rock careened off the canyon floor, knocking Uncle Steve's legs out from under him. I lunged forward and grabbed his pack, tugging him to safety.

The rockslide stopped as quickly as it started.

Uncle Steve was injured. Although he could stand up, he couldn't walk. Amy rushed to his side. She helped him sit down and then slid his pant leg up, revealing a contusion on his left calf muscle.

"Does it hurt here?" Amy asked, pressing gently on his ankle.

"Yeah!" he gasped.

"How's your foot?" Amy questioned.

"Foot is fine. But my ankle isn't so great," he added, trying to downplay the extent of his injury.

Amy felt around his ankle and closely examined his leg. "Well, it's not real bad; nothing is broken. However, I suggest that you keep your boot on and try walking around for a while. You have a sprained ankle. The boot will keep the swelling down and, if you walk around, you might be able to walk it off."

"It's not broken? That's good. A sprained ankle - shouldn't I put ice on it, raise it up, and stay off of it for a few days?" Uncle Steve asked.

"Oh, sure. And where is the ice machine? And do you think you *would* stay off of it for a few days? I really doubt that," Amy responded. "The treatment that I have suggested is what was used in the old days for ankle sprains for basketball players. It worked back then, it should work now. Keep the shoe on, which keeps the swelling minimized, walk on it to keep the blood flowing, and, in a day or so, you should be able to put your weight on it without it hurting…too much."

"So, what do you want me to do?" Uncle Steve asked. "Just wait here while you guys go find the field of flowers?"

"Yes, that is precisely what will have to happen. I'm your doctor and those are my orders," Amy insisted.

"You're an animal doctor!" Uncle Steve protested.

"Yes, and I'm the closest thing to a doctor out here. If you don't like my diagnosis, go get a second opinion!" Amy practically shouted.

Uncle Steve was silent. Amy was right and he knew it. He finally asked, "So, what's the plan, Doctor?"

"We have to climb up one of these pathways in order to find the mountaintop with yellow flowers. You can't climb, and it's too steep for Katie. So before Austin and I leave, we will set up our base camp here on the canyon floor. Now I suggest that we camp under this ledge. That way you won't have another close encounter with a boulder. Then we will head up the pathways. We don't know which mountain has the flowers, so it could take us awhile to find it."

Katie had been walking around the area while they were talking; she overheard what Amy had just said. Katie leaned over excitedly and motioned to us. "Hey, come here, you guys, I think we're closer than you think!" She was pointing to a golden-yellow plant laden with bright red berries.

* * * * *

Woodrow sat on the ledge, counting his blessings. The boulder had rocketed past him, missing him by a hair. He was lucky. An inch or so more, and he would have been smashed to smithereens on the canyon floor, along with all the other rocks.

"That was close!" Mr. Smith exclaimed, grasping his painful finger.

"That was too close," Woodrow agreed, his eyes wide with surprise that he hadn't fallen over the edge.

"This place is cursed, I tell you," Mr. Smith added, peering over the ledge.

"That's nonsense," insisted Calvin. "If it was cursed, then my brother would be my dead brother. So we don't have a curse. Let's get back to work."

The four men shifted their attention away from the canyon floor and back to the business at hand. They studied the next rock that needed to be removed, this one, thankfully, smaller in size. But they were worn out - not only from the strain of dislodging the massive rock, but also from their close call with the possibility of ending up flat as pancakes on the canyon floor.

"Well, that was easy," joked Calvin. "One down and two more to go. This next one is a little smaller than the last one. And we don't have to move it that far. Just over here." He pointed to the side of the entrance.

So the four men started once again to pry, shovel, slide, sweat, and anything else required in order to move the next rock. Woodrow decided to place his entire weight onto it. He pushed and pushed and finally, his shovel handle split. There was a loud, sharp cracking sound, then Woodrow lost his balance and fell to the ground, hitting his head on the rock. But that provided just enough pressure to loosen the rock. Mr. Jones grunted. Then, using his hands, arms and back, he got the rock to slide out of the way, just enough for Calvin to slip in behind it.

Calvin was now within arms' length of the golden statue. They all could see it. The gold statue stood about four feet high, glistening whenever the sun peeked through the clouds. Calvin was entranced with its beauty. He marveled at its golden luster. His fingers were desperately stretching to touch the golden prize, but the statue remained obstinately out of his reach. He wanted it badly. Badly!

"OK!" he shouted. "We're down to one shovel and one pickax. Don't break any more of the handles, you got it?" He was a man obsessed. "We've got just one big rock and a couple of smaller ones to move and then this gold mine is open for business!"

"We have just a couple of hours before dark," Mr. Jones reminded him. "We won't clear those last rocks in time and we can't climb down from these cliffs in the dark. I think we should go back to the hideout and come back tomorrow."

"And I'm hungry! Doesn't anyone want to get something to eat?" Mr. Smith added.

"Tomorrow morning we can get that last big one there. It looks like it will take a lot of time," Woodrow said.

Calvin wanted the gold, and he wanted it now! But he understood about trying to descend the mountain in the dark. And, he didn't want to reach the statue only to leave it fully exposed throughout the night. "Yeah, that's right. Let's come back tomorrow and finish the job," he agreed. "After we get that big one out, then it will be clear sailing." *Who knows, there may be some more golden surprises further inside the gold mine,* he thought.

"Did you hear something?" asked Mr. Smith.

"Like what?" asked Calvin, looking around.

"I don't know," Mr. Smith conceded. "It sounded like a rustling or a growl."

"Yeah, that was my stomach," Calvin said. "I'm hungry, let's get out of here." He wanted to get to the cave before everybody else, so he told Mr. Jones to gather up all the tools. Then he headed toward the path that led back down to the hideout.

Mr. Smith looked at Woodrow. "You sure you didn't hear something?" he asked.

"I thought I heard something awhile ago. Sounded like a growling noise," Woodrow admitted.

They watched Calvin as he scrambled down the path.

Woodrow added, "Maybe it's part of the curse."

"There may be something to this curse," Mr. Smith acknowledged. Then he looked directly at Woodrow. "Hey, what's wrong with your eye?"

Woodrow touched the side of his face gingerly. "Ouch! This must have happened when my shovel broke and I slammed into that rock."

"It looks like it's going to be a real shiner," Mr. Smith observed, examining the red, swollen, lump protruding from just above Woodrow's eyebrow.

"It's all part of the curse," Woodrow solemnly insisted.

"You mean like ghosts and stuff?" Mr. Smith asked as he watched Mr. Jones carry the tools to the hideout.

Woodrow was wide-eyed (well, at least one eye was wide), and he nodded emphatically.

"Let's get out of here," Mr. Smith urged, looking around nervously. He and Woodrow hastily followed Mr. Jones down the path.

Calvin was the first to arrive at the hideout. He checked to make sure that the other men were nowhere in sight, then he walked directly to Mr.

Jones's bedroll. He tugged roughly at the blanket until his gun dropped on the floor. Calvin had surreptitiously watched Mr. Jones conceal the gun inside his bedroll that morning. Now, he had it back. Calvin calmly picked up the gun and tucked it into his trousers. He would find an opportunity to load the bullets later. He purposefully pulled his shirt over his pants to ensure that no one would notice the gun peeking out from his waistband. Having the gun reunited with its rightful owner gave Calvin a strong sense of security.

The rest of the men arrived at the hideout, and Calvin suggested that Woodrow and Mr. Smith prepare dinner. He was hungry and he felt that those two needed something to do that would keep them both out of trouble.

Mr. Jones tended to the fire, which was now generating some serious flames. Coffee was being brewed directly over the fire. The aroma of freshly brewed coffee on top of the burning wood stimulated the men's hearty appetites.

However, the smell didn't linger only inside the cave. The smoke and the aroma of the coffee drifted outside, seeming to permeate the area.

This did not go unnoticed.

* * * * *

Amy and I were climbing up the side of the mountain when I suddenly stopped.

"Amy, am I imagining things or do I smell coffee?" I asked.

"I've been smelling coffee, too," Amy replied. "We're too high up for it to be coming from our camp. It must be coming from another camp. We need to be careful."

We had stopped on a pathway that seemed as if it would take us east for a little bit before leading us up the mountain again. Since up the mountain was the direction that we wanted to go, we followed the path.

Amy noticed there was smoke emanating from a cave that was just around the corner. "Austin, carry Sarah and take the two-way radio. I'll turn it off in case we get an untimely call. Sarah is in a real bad way and we don't need to get slowed down by anybody who might be here." She paused to look back at the cave and the smoke.

"I'll take the lead and I want you to follow close behind me, but not too close. If someone comes out of one of those caves and sees us, hide. I'm bigger than you and can probably block their view of you if you stay behind me. If that happens, I want you to take Sarah and the radio and crawl up that pathway." She pointed up the mountain. "Then you get Sarah up to that field and get her well again, OK?"

"But what happens if these are bad people?" I asked worriedly.

"I've dealt with people like Mr. Pickett for a long time. I can take care of myself. I just can't take care of Sarah, too. So I need you to do that for me, OK?" she requested.

I grudgingly agreed.

Amy was aware of my misgivings. "Look, Austin, if anybody comes out they'll probably ask me some questions. I'll tell them my base camp is in the canyon and that I am to report back to them tomorrow. They won't do anything but hold me up for awhile. I'll be fine. Are you OK with that?"

I nodded in agreement as I looked around to make sure that no one was coming.

"If I'm not up there by tonight, once you have Sarah on the road to recovery, call Steve. Remember, you have the two-way radio and you can get some help. But I'm sure that won't be necessary. OK?"

I nodded again.

"But we have to get Sarah to that field," Amy reminded me. "Now let's get going."

Amy and I slowly made our way along the pathway; we could see the narrow passage winding up the mountain. The path was getting closer.

We were within ten feet and things were looking good.

Amy had just reached the path, when all of the sudden...

"Hey, who are you?" shouted a very surprised Calvin.

Amy stood up and motioned behind her back for me to start climbing up the narrow pathway. She wanted to give me some time to get away, so she slowly walked towards Calvin, trying to prevent him from seeing me.

I noticed Amy feel for her knife, which was at her side. She continued to approach Calvin and I heard her say, "Hi, I'm with the Park and Recreation Department – we're scouting the area today."

Amy again motioned for me to leave. I reluctantly turned and climbed the narrow path.

* * * * *

Calvin stood silently as he watched approaching figure warily. He looked around, but didn't see anyone else.

Amy continued, "We have a base camp on the floor of the canyon and several of us are scouting. I was chosen to scout this wall. Is everything all right?"

"Oh yeah. Everything is just great," Calvin said. "You just startled me for a moment. How long will your group be looking at this area?"

Amy looked around, assuring herself that Austin was nowhere in sight. "Oh, just today, then we'll be leaving the area. You know, off to scout another area."

"Oh yeah, I can imagine how that is. Well, why don't you just go on your way and we will mind our business, too," Calvin said, hoping she would just leave.

At that moment, Mr. Jones stepped out of the hideout.

He looked at Amy and she saw him at the same time. Her startled look immediately gave away the fact that she recognized him.

Mr. Jones pointed at her. "I know you."

Calvin, always on his toes, realized that something wasn't right. He grabbed the gun concealed in his trousers and pointed it at Amy. "Well, I don't know you, but I plan to. Get her knife," he ordered Mr. Jones, "and then get her inside."

Calvin looked around once again to make certain no one else was around. Once satisfied, he followed Amy and Mr. Jones into the cave.

"Look who we have here," Mr. Jones said, directing his comment to Mr. Smith.

Mr. Smith looked up and saw Amy. "What's she doing here?" he yelled, pointing his swollen finger at Amy. "Do you know how I have been traumatized ever since you had those animals attack me?"

Amy stared at Mr. Smith and Mr. Jones. She remembered them very well and realized she was in trouble. She couldn't pretend not to know them, so she repeated what she had said earlier. "There are several of us and we have a base camp on the floor of the canyon and…" She casually walked towards the cave entrance, hoping to get away, as she continued talking. "…several of us are scouting. I was chosen to scout this wall…"

"Sit down," Mr. Jones commanded, moving hastily to get between Amy and the cave's entrance. "You aren't going anywhere."

Calvin stared. "OK, who is this and how do you know her?"

Mr. Smith and Mr. Jones offered a brief summary of their last encounter with Amy back in Mountview. Of course, they left out the really embarrassing parts.

Calvin looked at Amy. "Sit down there and don't make any noise."

Amy was in trouble - she knew it, but at the moment, she couldn't do anything about it. She was aware of the probability that if she yelled, Austin would hear her and would try to help her. He had a job to do - he needed to save Sarah. She also couldn't contact Steve; she had given the two-way to Austin. And, even if Steve knew that she was in trouble, his ankle was in bad shape and he wouldn't be able to do anything to help her. She did the only thing she *could* do - sit on the floor with her back to the cave wall facing the fire, and think.

"So, you think there could be more of them?" Calvin asked. He was on his feet and headed outside before Mr. Smith was able to respond.

* * * *

I was carrying Sarah, which was like carrying a sack of potatoes around my neck. The two-way radio was banging against the rocks, my body was banging against the rocks, but Sarah wasn't banging...I kept her in front of me and absorbed the bumping with my body. It seemed like I was making a lot of noise, but apparently not, because when I looked back, no one was following me. I couldn't see Amy and I hoped she was all right.

I shifted Sarah's sling to my right side. That gave me my entire left arm to use to climb the rocks. I finally reached the next ridge where I rested for a minute. Then I stood up and looked down, hoping I'd be able to see something.

That was a mistake.

Right at the very moment that I was looking down, Calvin was looking up. "Hey, you up there!" he shouted, racing to the path that led up the mountain.

I had to get going, and I mean fast. I slipped and bashed my knee.

"Ouch!" I yelled.

I got back up on my feet and started climbing the last stage of the mountain.

Calvin was gaining on me.

My two-way was slamming into the rocks as I arrived at the narrowest part of the climb. I was sliding and slamming and making a whole lot of noise.

Too much noise...

The commotion was too much for the alpha mountain lion that lived inside the gold mine. The dislodging of the rocks earlier in the day had given this two hundred pound beast just enough room to slide through the opening at the very top of the cave. The mountain lion dug his way out of the cave through an entrance that had been closed for hundreds of years. Once out, he listened intently for the source of the racket, honing in on his prey...

...which was me!

* * * * *

The source of the noise was about to enter the field of the yellow flowers…and the mountain lion couldn't let that happen.

He bounded from the rocks and raced towards the narrow path that would take him to the top - that familiar narrow path that the mountain lion had traveled so many times in his long life.

Once the beast reached the pathway he discovered the source of the noise. It was a human who had just reached the summit. The mountain lion was determined to catch and destroy this intruder. He bounded up the path, covering a distance of ten feet with every jump.

Calvin was so close that he nearly screamed in terror when he first saw the golden cat streaking by. Fortunately, he kept silent. The mountain lion didn't see him…at least not at that moment. Calvin crouched down low and prayed that he wouldn't be seen.

Calvin cautiously craned his neck to see the huge beast reach the summit and vanish, probably running towards the person that he had seen looking down at him. *Ha*, he thought. *That guy is dead meat right about now.* He laughed again to himself. He needed to remain quiet – after all, if there was one mountain lion, there were probably others.

Calvin sensed that the coast was clear and decided to return to the cave - very quietly.

That poor son-of-a-gun reached a fate a lot worse than whatever I was going to do to him. He laughed again…still to himself.

"So, you had a partner out there, did ya?" he asked Amy.

"There are members of my party all over this place," she replied.

"Well, if you noticed, I used the past tense." Calvin paused for dramatic effect. "Since you have one less partner now."

"What do you mean?" Amy asked apprehensively.

"What I mean is this - the last time I saw your buddy, he was running for his life. Why? Because there was a two-hundred pound mountain lion running after him. That's why. Oh, it was great." Calvin laughed again, this time, out loud. "I hate to be the one to tell you this, but I don't think he'll make it. In fact, right now he's probably the main course."

Amy's mouth dropped open in shock, then she closed her eyes. She tried to reassure herself that Austin was unharmed. "No, he'll be fine," she said defiantly.

"Oh, I'm sure he's just fine. He'll be finely chewed up into tiny little pieces - that's how fine he is," Calvin sneered. "Don't you like my sense of humor? Oh well. Listen up everyone - be on the lookout for those mountain lions. They're big and mean and they are hungry…well, I know one that isn't. Ha, ha, ha."

Chapter 16

I was running for my life.

I looked behind me. There was the largest animal that I had ever seen, charging at me, gaining ground with every leap. I was running so fast, looking for a place to hide, that I almost tripped. As I caught myself, I suddenly realized that I was in the golden field of flowers. This was an open field - there was no place to hide.

I knew that there was no escape. Running was futile. I slowed down to a walk and glanced back. The cat had slowed down, too. He must have known that I wasn't going anywhere.

He had me and he wasn't in any hurry.

I stopped and turned to look directly at the huge beast. He also stopped. We both knew that he could finish me at any moment, so what was the use of running?

Then the cat began to circle me. He slowly moved to the right – keeping his eyes on me at all times.

I watched him move powerfully, confidently. Every muscle in his body rippled as he stalked me. His eyes penetrated right through me and I felt a chill go up and down my spine. The race was over and we both knew it. He was sizing me up, determining how to finish me off.

I suddenly remembered something Mr. Baker had told us when we were at the Western North Carolina Nature Center. He had said that cats like the chase. That's why they always attack from the rear. I had forgotten that bit of information. Boy, did it come in handy now.

I was still holding Sarah in the sling. She was in desperate need of the food and nourishment that these flowers could provide. I could see that her tail had already changed to a beaver's tail and her ears were sticking straight up like a rabbit's ears. She looked like she was unconscious and, for a moment, I completely forgot about the mountain lion. Right before my eyes, Sarah's paws were turning into furry little bear paws. White spots were suddenly breaking out all over her stomach! I watched the transformation, transfixed. Sarah was now completely in the form of a Schmooney. I quickly bent down and picked up a clump of leaves. Sarah finally woke up and noticed the leaves in my hand. At first, she ate slowly. Then she began to eat faster. I looked up to keep my eye on the mountain lion. He had stopped in his tracks and was now staring at us. Sarah had finished the first part of her meal and was eager for more. She wanted down. So I gently lowered her out of the sling and she rolled to the ground where she immediately proceeded to gorge herself.

When I looked up again, I discovered that the mountain lion was sitting down, just watching Sarah and me! What was he up to? I was sure that at any moment we would be dinner for him.

And then I noticed stealthy movements to my right.

Oh my! I turned my full attention in that direction. There was another mountain lion. And then another. And another. They were coming through the woods behind us and heading directly towards me.

So that's what he was up to. He had just been waiting for his friends. *Am I going to be the main course for dinner tonight?* I wondered.

I was terrified, but at the same time, I managed to think clearly.

I glanced down at Sarah, who was gobbling her way through the field. She didn't even seem to be aware of the danger we were in.

I figured it would be all over soon.

That's when I heard it! A deep male voice was asking, *'Who are you?'*

I looked around, searching for another human being. But no one else was up here. I noticed that the first big lion was still watching me. The others gathered around him and faced me.

What is going on now? I thought.

And then I heard it once again.

'Who are you? Why are you here?' the voice repeated.

I sent, *'I'm here so that my friend will live. She needs to eat these flowers to stay alive.'*

'These flowers are deadly. This is not a safe place for you to be,' the male voice informed me.

I sent, *'My friend is a Schmooney and eating these flowers will save her life.'*

The majestic mountain lion rose to his feet. He approached me guardedly.

I decided to act on my hunch so I sent, *'Am I talking to you - the one that is approaching me?'*

'Yes, you are,' he replied.

'Am I in danger?' I asked.

'Yes, you are,' he answered again. *'But not from me and not from my family.'*

He was suddenly next to me, having watched my every movement since he began his approach. He sniffed me and looked me over. Once satisfied that I posed no threat to him, he looked down at Sarah.

I suddenly was filled with an overpowering sensation of love. I know that sounds weird. But it wasn't my love for the cat; it was his love for Sarah that was coming through to me.

Sarah looked up, her mouth stuffed with leaves. She stopped, and the two stared at each other. Then I heard the words that changed my life forever. Sarah swallowed and looked deep into the majestic cat's eyes. *'Grandfather?'*

'Yes, my child. I can't believe it is you.' He rubbed his head affectionately against her body. This, of course, caused Sarah to fall down. He then opened his mouth and picked her up by the scruff of her neck, setting her back on her feet.

'I am still a bit weak,' she confessed.

'Come, have your friend carry you to my home. It will be very safe there for both of you.' And with that, Sarah climbed into my arms and we followed the lions to the back of the field.

I know that I was tired. I must have been very tired. Why wasn't I trembling with fear? I don't really know the answer to that question. I wasn't afraid. And I am not particularly brave. So I have no idea why I wasn't scared.

I should have been afraid. I should have been terrified! After all, I had been chased by men, then chased by mountain lions, and now, I found myself talking to one. Why wasn't I afraid?

I should know by now to expect the unexpected. Nothing should really surprise me anymore. But this definitely should have.

It was getting dark and it was especially hard to see under the trees. When we reached the back trail, there was just enough light for us to climb down the pathway safely. Fortunately, this path was much easier than the other ones we had been on.

We descended the path and reached a ridge. We traversed the ridge, which led to an entrance into another cave. Once inside the cave, it was so dark that I couldn't even see my own hand in front of my face so I sent, *'I can't see where I'm going.'*

Sarah replied, *'Don't worry, I can see fine.'*

So Sarah became like my seeing-eye dog. Talk about having trust in someone. I carried her and she told me when to stop and where to step and what to avoid. It wasn't long until we heard the command: *We can rest here. This is safe.*

Before, I had been able to see a little, but now we were completely in pitch-black darkness. So I sent, *'You mean you all can really see in this blackness?'*

The male sent, *'We can see movement and we can see objects. Don't worry, you are safe where you are.'* He continued, *'It would not be wise for you and Sarah to venture any further back in this cave. There is a mother, Claire, and her cubs are back there. Claire will protect her children at all costs. So don't go back there. Heck, none of us go back there. These mothers really get to be a pain sometimes.'*

I felt better. He was funny. Funny? How could that be? Wild animals telling jokes? I have so much to learn.

Then I remembered Amy and sent, *'Sarah and I have friends nearby. One of them is a girl named Amy. She was...'* I searched for the right word, *'...captured by some bad people and may be in danger. Is there anyway that I can go save her?'*

The male replied, *'There are some men that have been moving rocks outside our home. I went to investigate the noise and that is when I saw you. The cave that you are now in, leads to that area where they are working, but it is on the other side of the mountain. There is a cave below this one and it, too, has an opening on the other side of the mountain. Perhaps she is in that cave. I can send one of my friends to go see. Do you want my friend to scare them? Or maybe eat them?'*

'Eat them?' I sent back frantically. *'What do you mean, eat them?'*

'I was just kidding. You need to have a sense of humor, young man. What is your name?'

'Austin,' I sent. I suddenly remembered that I had my survival gear with me. I felt around inside my pack for my light stick. I shook it and suddenly, a warm glow filled the room. I could finally see, just like the rest of them and I noticed that the large lion was staring at the light in fascination.

'I have never seen that done before – you must be very powerful, Austin,' he sent.

'It's just a light stick,' I informed him modestly. *'What **will** you do to those men though?'*

'I was only kidding about the eating part. But seriously, I will send my friend to go scare them - you know, growl and hiss?'

'Really? You do that for fun?' I asked.

'Sometimes,' he replied nonchalantly.

'Wow! No, we don't need to scare them yet. I just want to know if Amy is all right. She could be in some real danger. She might be the only girl in there. But if there are others, Amy is wearing a green jacket and a green hat. You can't miss her,' I explained.

'I will send one of my friends,' he promised.

And with that, something happened. It was hard for me to tell what was going on in the shadows of the cave, but I did hear a growl or two.

Sarah sent, *'I am feeling much better but I am still very tired. I want to sleep. There is so much to learn. Can we talk tomorrow?'*

'Sure,' I sent. But I felt that the message wasn't for me.

The male sent, *'Get a good night's sleep, Sarah. Austin, you are very safe here. You both are, even though it is dark. Try to sleep. We have a lot to do tomorrow. We will know something very soon about Amy. I asked my friend Aiden, to go check on her. And, by the way, please call me Rex.'*

Then I remembered the two-way radio and that Amy had turned it off. *'Mr. Rex, may I call my other friends who are camped in the canyon? They will want to know that I'm safe.'*

'My name is Rex, not Mr. Rex. And if you call your friends, you will be talking out loud and the other lions will hear you. That would not be a good thing. Before you do that, let me go back to tell everyone that they are safe, too.'

That made sense to me.

Once he moved away from the small glow provided by my light stick, I could no longer see him. Nor could I hear him – mountain lions move so quietly. But I felt Sarah, who was cuddled up against my legs. She was fast asleep and that made me feel comfortable and warm. Rex returned so stealthily that I didn't even realize it until he sent, *'It is safe for you to talk to your friends, but do so quickly and quietly.'*

I had been trying to figure out what to tell Uncle Steve. Amy wasn't with me, and I currently wasn't in a position to find her. But I didn't want to worry my uncle since he wouldn't be able to – and shouldn't even try to – attempt to climb the mountain with his injured leg.

The light was growing dimmer and I figured I didn't really need it now. I remembered that when the two-way was turned on, each button was backlit, which meant that the keys would illuminate. I finally found the 'on/off' switch. First, I located the volume control and turned it low. Then I pressed the 'on' button. The radio lit up. In the pitch black, the lights on the radio glowed like a torch.

Wow! The radio was casting really cool shadows against the wall. The light shined on one of the lions and his mouth opened wide in disgust. Whoops! I better not do that again.

I found and pressed the key button.

"Uncle Steve, this is Austin." I waited.

"Austin, is everything all right?" Uncle Steve quickly responded.

"Yes," I said. "Everything seems to be fine. Sarah has eaten, she's much better, and she's fast asleep now. I'm safe in a cave." I hesitated for a second. I really didn't want to worry him. And I was pretty sure it was true, so I added, "And Amy is safe in another cave."

"What? Why two different caves?" he asked.

I had to tell him something and I really didn't want to lie. But I didn't want him hobbling off in the middle of the night trying to climb the mountain with a leg that wouldn't support him. So I tried to keep to the truth as much as I could without giving anything away. "I'm with a pack of mountain lions and perfectly safe. Sarah is apparently related to one of them. Amy is in another cave and Rex has sent Aiden to look in on her. I know this sounds really weird, but I'm sure you're used to it by now. We're all safe," I said with all the assurance I could muster.

There was silence on the other end. I waited and waited. Then I pressed the key again. "Did you hear what I said?"

"Uh, yes, Katie and I heard you." There was more silence. "We're glad that you're doing well. And we hope that you haven't been eating the flowers, because you are saying some weird things. Who are Rex and Aiden?"

I smiled. "They're new friends of ours. We're fine. Good night – we'll see you tomorrow. I love you."

"Same here, Austin. I love you, too. Good night."

I turned the radio off. After a few moments, Rex sent, *'Are they safe?'*

'Yes, sir, they are both safe.'

I heard something rush through the entrance. I guessed that it was Aiden. Rex sent, *'Aiden is back.'* There was silence for a moment, before he added, *'Your friend is all right. She is next to a fire and looks fine. There are four men in the cave with her and she does not appear to be in danger. She was eating something when he looked in on her.'*

'Thank you,' I sent. *'And please thank Aiden. I'm going to sleep now.'*

'Good night,' Rex sent.

I closed my eyes and slept so soundly that I don't think a rocket landing next to my head would have woken me up. I was definitely tired.

The next morning, I awoke with Sarah still asleep at my feet. She had kept me warm all night. She looked good. She seemed to be healthy.

Light was now splashing through the cave, although long shadows coated the walls. I could see a large open area where I noticed three cats sleeping in curled-up positions scattered around the room. I looked towards the dark end of the cave but knew better than to go back in that area. Uncle Steve had always told me ***never*** go near any animal when her babies are present.

Considering the fact that I had slept on the floor of a dark, damp cave all night, surrounded by man-eating mountain lions and basically not able to see anything or, for that matter, hear anything, I was surprisingly well-rested.

Now I needed to turn my attention to Amy.

I realized Rex was sending a message to me, although I wasn't sure where he was. *'The bad men are already working at the entrance of the cave.'*

'How do I get there?' I asked.

'You can't, without being noticed,' he replied.

Then I heard Sarah. *'I can.'*

Rex was on his way back to the cave to meet with Sarah and me. I looked over at Sarah who was on her side, waving one of her bear arms at me. *'Good morning, Austin.'*

'You look rested. I'm getting tired of carrying you around all the time,' I joked. *'Are you ready to go out and earn your keep?'*

'You bet,' she sent. Then she got up and rubbed affectionately against my leg.

'That will get you nowhere,' I teased.

She looked around. *'Where's Amy?'*

I explained the situation until Rex arrived.

'Good morning to both of you. Sarah - is what they call you?' Rex asked.

'Yes, I am now Sarah. And this is Austin.' She pointed to me.

I held up my hand up and waved.

'This is my grandfather,' Sarah sent, looking at Rex.

I knew that from last night, so I wasn't completely knocked off-guard, as I had been when I first heard this little piece of information. I decided to say something clever. *'I can see the family resemblance.'*

Rex laughed. It kind of a low, rumbling laugh. But it wasn't like an African lion and it wasn't like Carrie the Cougar. It was soft, but commanding. I liked his sense of humor. I have always said that if you are going to have a ferocious mountain lion around you, you might as well have one with a good sense of humor. Well, maybe I never actually said that. But it *is* definitely a good thing.

Rex sent, *'There is a lot to talk about, but first, let's help your friend Amy.'*

I'm ready for that, I replied. *What's the plan?*

So we prepared a plan. And it was a good plan. But we were going to need a bit of luck - and a bunch of skill. I just hoped that Uncle Steve was still the best shot in the county.

Sarah and I went to the field. She ate some more leaves and gathered a bunch of berries. Next, I tore off a sleeve from my shirt, tied one end of the sleeve so it was closed, forming a handy pouch where Sarah could carry the berries. Then we returned to the cave.

Another one of our new lion friends, Kai, was to be Sarah's guide. They left together to travel the back way into the hideout, where the four men slept and ate. There were two parts to this rescue plan. The first part was to find Amy. The second part was to put the berries into the men's coffee pot, the results of which would keep them occupied for quite awhile. Then, if Amy was able to get out of there, Sarah and Kai would bring her safely back here to us.

* * * * *

Sarah and Kai silently went through the back entrance to the men's hideout and approached the front of the cave cautiously. It was dark, but they both could navigate safely.

They saw Amy sitting on the floor with only one man watching her. They watched from the shadows, remaining undetected. Since the fire was smoldering without any flames, Sarah figured she would be able to sneak over to the open coffee pot and deposit the berries inside. The bubbling water would boil the juice from the berries and lace the coffee with extreme potency. Whoever drank the coffee would then be in for major intestinal eruptions, meaning they would be severely incapacitated and unable to chase anyone anywhere.

Sarah approached the fire, aware that the man had his back turned slightly away from her. She lifted her little bear arm and stealthily dropped the berries into the coffee. Since Amy was sitting with her back to the wall, she was facing the fire, when she suddenly noticed Sarah. Amy realized what was about to happen and knew she had to make sure that Mr. Smith didn't see Sarah. She cleared her throat. "Hey, you, let's talk about something. I'm bored."

Mr. Smith pointed his grossly misshapen and throbbing finger at her. "I told you, I am not talking to you. You had those little squirrels biting me like crazy when I was back there in Mountview. I will never forgive you. I still have nightmares about them."

Amy watched Sarah's arm continue to drop the berries into the pot. She looked at Mr. Smith. "Oh, come on, a big man like you. Those little squirrels didn't really hurt you, did they?"

Mr. Smith nodded vehemently. "Yes they did! And I'm going to stay mad."

That was all the time they needed. Sarah winked at Amy and slowly backed into the darkness to join Kai. The only thing left to do was let nature take its course.

Chapter 17

I was on the two-way radio talking with Uncle Steve.

"Let me explain a little more about last night," I began. I knew I had a lot of explaining to do, but I also knew where our focus needed to be at this moment. "Amy is being held hostage by some bad men in a cave about fifty feet above you. We're going to get her back. So there's no need for you to worry.

"We're working with some friendly mountain lions. So, if you see one, or two, or maybe even more of them, please don't shoot or cause them any harm because they're the good guys. They're friendly and they know that you're friendly, too. I'll explain the details later. Trust me on this one, please," I begged.

"Now, what we need you to do is this: You'll need to have your rifle ready. I don't really know what will happen, but the bad guys have at least one gun. You may need to help us out by using your rifle to protect us. I know that I'm probably not explaining this very well, but I really don't know what's going to happen or what to expect. And that's all you can really do from where you are. I'll explain the rest later. I promise."

"You're the man, Austin. I'll help any way that I can. Please be careful, OK?" Uncle Steve paused for a moment. I was thinking I should say something when he added, "And I can't wait to hear all about it. Good luck and be safe."

* * * * *

Back at the gold mine, Calvin, Woodrow, and Mr. Jones were moving the last rock out of the way. The Golden Gato was about to be revealed. They grunted and groaned and used every tool that they had to get the rock to budge. With a giant thud, the boulder grudgingly gave way, giving the men just enough space to enter the cave.

Calvin was the first to squeeze through the opening. "Here it is, men!" Calvin announced triumphantly, running his hands possessively over the statue. He tried to lift it, but it was solid gold, meaning it was extremely heavy and not at all willing to yield to his best efforts.

The other two men made their way inside and stopped in their tracks when their eyes fell on the statue. They marveled at the imposing work of solid gold as it glimmered in the sunlight, calling forth their every desire. It was magnificent. The men's thoughts ran rampant, seductive visions of their wildest dreams of riches, power and importance swirling around them.

A wonderful feeling overpowered the men for that moment. And, that moment was all the time that Calvin needed to put an abrupt end to those dreams. He pulled the gun from his trousers and pointed it at Mr. Jones. "You didn't really think that you could hide my gun from me, did you? You seemed to have made a rookie mistake there, Mr. Jones. And that will cost you – dearly," Calvin smirked.

"What I want you to do is this - Woodrow here is going to take the gun and walk you back to the hideout. He is going to fill a bag of things that I need and he will come back here…alone. You and your friend and that park ranger will stay in the cave until we come back for you. If you stick your head out of the cave, I will drop a lighted stick of dynamite on you from up here. Do you understand?" Calvin asked.

"Why are you doing this?" Mr. Jones wondered. "There's enough for all of us. You'll need our help carrying it down the mountain. You need us."

"Why, you ask? Because we can, that's why. I have the gun. I have the bullets. I have the gold. I make the rules," Calvin said contemptuously. "Now get going! Woodrow, take this gun and don't let either of them get the best of you. I will stay here with the gold. I won't let it out of my sight. Now go!" Calvin yelled as he stroked the golden statue.

Woodrow pointed the gun at Mr. Jones's back. They traveled slowly and carefully down the path and then walked across the ridge that led to the hideout. Amy was still sitting with her back against the wall when they entered the cave. Mr. Smith was pouring himself another cup of coffee.

"Well, it's about time you finally got here," Mr. Smith remarked, sipping a piping hot cup of berry-laced coffee. He raised the cup to his lips, only to freeze when he noticed Woodrow with a gun pointed in his direction.

Woodrow waved the gun in the air, trying to exude great authority. "I want you two to get over against that wall and stay there."

He then ordered Amy to get up and told her to put several specific items in the bag. As she followed his instructions, she asked if he wanted a cup of coffee.

"No!" he snapped nervously. "Just do as you are told."

Amy packed all the items into the bag. Then she had an idea. "Well, how about a cup of coffee for Mr. Jones here?" She picked up a cup, walked to the fire, and poured coffee into the cup. "Woodrow, would it be OK for them to sit on the floor now?"

Woodrow reluctantly agreed. Both Mr. Smith and Mr. Jones sank to the floor of the cave and sipped their berry-laced coffee in silence.

Amy was pleased. She thought, *Two down and one more to go.*

She then turned her attention back to Woodrow. "So, what's the plan there, Woodrow? You've got all the stuff and you got the gun, so what's next?" she asked, approaching him slowly.

Woodrow was rifling through the bag, making sure all the items were packed, while occasionally looking up to see where everyone was. When he realized Amy was coming towards him, he barked, "You better stop right there!"

"OK, OK. I'll stop here. Hey, are you sure you don't want a cup of coffee? It's real good," Amy said pleasantly, while picking up a cup and backing up towards the coffee pot.

Woodrow yelled, "No, I told you! I don't even like coffee!"

"OK, OK, I'll keep this cup for myself," Amy said.

"Just sit right there and let me finish," Woodrow commanded. "I've got to do this right."

Amy obediently lowered herself to the floor and glanced over at Mr. Smith and Mr. Jones, wondering if they were suffering any ill effects yet.

Much to her delight, Mr. Smith had set his cup down and was rubbing his stomach. That was a good sign. They were both real quiet. That, too, was a good sign.

A few moments later, Mr. Jones dropped his cup and started looking around the room…searching for something.

Amy thought, *I bet he's looking for a bathroom and a Sears Catalog.*

She looked over at Woodrow. She wasn't sure if he had been sent down there to keep them company, keep them quiet, or worse… After all, he ***did*** have a gun.

Mr. Smith rolled over. "Oh, my stomach!" he groaned.

Woodrow stared at him, not comprehending what was happening.

Mr. Jones suddenly grabbed his stomach and cried out in agony, "Oh, my!" He remained doubled over, unable to straighten up.

Woodrow wanted to get away from these crazy men. While clutching the gun, he was attempting to lift the bag, which was now very heavy, onto his arm. This was nearly impossible to do with only one hand. He put the gun down and slung the bag over his shoulder.

That was the perfect opportunity for Kai to leap out of the darkness. Bone-chilling growls filled the air as he leapt directly towards a terrified Woodrow.

Amy shrieked!

Mr. Smith and Mr. Jones grunted, but they had more pressing issues on their minds.

Woodrow reacted with surprising speed. There was no time to pick up the gun. He ran with blind instinct from the cave towards the pathway that would lead him up to the gold mine, which he hoped would provide safe haven. The weight of the bag didn't seem to slow him down at all. In one fluid motion, he was gone.

Sarah walked towards the center of the cave and she called to Kai, who immediately returned to her side to protect her.

Amy raced over to Sarah and they embraced.

Meanwhile, Woodrow scrambled up the mountain with great alacrity. His bag continuously smashed against the rock wall, and he screamed as he lost his footing several times along the pathway.

When Calvin saw his brother, he groaned and wondered, *Oh no, what happened this time?* He yelled, "What's wrong?"

Woodrow was still flying up the pathway, gasping for breath. Calvin received no response.

"What's wrong, Woodrow?" he shouted again.

"There's a mountain lion in the cave and it's eating everybody!" Woodrow shrieked. He had now arrived at the ridge, and he was racing pell-mell towards Calvin.

Calvin put out his arms to slow Woodrow down. "Hey, settle down, slow down. It's OK."

"Did you hear me? There's a mountain lion down there and he's eating everyone!" Woodrow was wide-eyed, except for his right eye, which still bore the marks of his encounter with the rock.

"Hey, that's all right. Heck, that's perfect. This means we have fewer things to take care of – fewer witnesses. Relax, Woodrow," Calvin reassured him. "Now, go into the cave and start breaking the statue apart. I'll put the finishing touches on the entrance to that cave below us. Start putting the gold in the bags that you brought up here. You *did* bring the bags, right? I'll take just this stick of dynamite and say goodbye to our problems."

Woodrow held the bags up for Calvin to see. "You're going to blow up the entrance with dynamite?"

"Of course, how else do you think I can seal the cave entrance? Now, just go in there and do what you're told." Calvin patted his brother on his arm and pointed him toward the gold mine. "I plan on sealing the deal. I'm going to light a stick of dynamite and seal their tomb," he chortled as he reached into his pocket and produced a match. "Hold your ears…Calvin is about to close the door!"

* * * * *

What Calvin didn't know was that Woodrow wasn't the only one who could hear him. I was on the ridge above them and, as I leaned down, I was able to hear everything they said. Rex was standing next to me. I sent, *'He plans on using dynamite to seal the entrance. We must stop him.'*

'What are you going to do?' Rex sent.

I stood at the very edge of the ridge and peered down. I could see Calvin - he was about to light the dynamite! I didn't have time to plan – my mind was racing furiously.

The two-way radio suddenly crackled to life. Fortunately, I still had the volume turned way down. I heard Uncle Steve say, "Austin, don't move." I couldn't think of anything except, *I hope Uncle Steve is still the best shot in the county.*

Calvin walked to the edge of the cliff and looked down at the hideout entrance.

"Sweet dreams, friends," he cackled, as he lit the dynamite.

Rex suddenly let out a terrifying growl, which reverberated all the way down to the canyon floor. It startled me, and horrified Calvin.

Calvin's head shot up to find an enormous mountain lion looming threateningly above him. Then he saw me standing by the side of this deadly predator. I waved.

Calvin's cocky expression transformed from confidence to confusion. He tilted his head to one side. His mouth opened slightly. For a moment, Calvin must have forgotten that he had a lighted stick of dynamite in his hand. He looked directly at me, and I could see shock and bewilderment filling his eyes. It's not every day that you see a killer mountain lion standing calmly next to a young boy, looking down at you from fifty feet above. That moment, that precise moment, was all the time that Uncle Steve needed.

A shot rang out.

Bang!

The sound echoed through the canyon.

A bullet tore into Calvin's right arm - the same arm with the hand that was holding the dynamite. The force of the bullet's impact completely spun Calvin around. The rapidly burning dynamite catapulted to the ground directly outside of the opening to the hole-in-the-mountain, disappearing from our sight.

Woodrow heard the shot. He looked over to see his brother clutch his arm in agony, as bright red blood splashed onto the rocky floor.

Calvin was in shock. Perhaps it was shock from seeing Rex and me. Or, perhaps it was the shock of having a bullet pierce his body causing his bright, red blood to flow out of his arm. Or, perhaps it was the shock of seeing the lighted dynamite lying extremely close to where he was standing, about to explode in mere seconds.

Whatever caused the shock, Calvin could not stop staring at the hole in his arm, as he tried to apply enough pressure to get his blood to stop spilling all over the place.

Woodrow, fearing for his brother's life, raced out of the cave with the same speed that he had earlier exhibited. Woodrow wrapped his large, strong arms around Calvin. He noticed the dynamite and realized that the fuse was dangerously short, meaning that the dynamite would explode at any moment. He dragged his wounded brother back into the cave with animal force.

I thought I might hear Woodrow's voice trying to help his wounded brother.

But instead, I only heard Calvin who was yelling at his brother at the top of his lungs, acutely aware that the dynamite was about to detonate. He was ordering a different course of action. He probably realized that the force of the blast would seal the entrance to the gold mine.

He also probably realized that his brother, with his final misguided gesture of good will, had dragged him into what was about to become a tomb that would seal their fate forever.

Who knows what went through Calvin's mind in those last few seconds?

The blast was enormous.

BAM!

The canyon walls echoed with the force of the explosion. The rocks began to slide and I realized that the ground was shifting under my feet. Rex grabbed my arm in his mouth and yanked me towards the center of the field.

He saved my life.

The explosion rocked the side of the mountain, which precipitated a major landslide. The area where I had been standing disappeared down the mountain. The blast brought small stones and large boulders down in heavy streams, sealing the front entrance of the gold mine. Heavy rocks tumbled over those that now sealed the front of the gold mine, plummeting down onto the lower ridge. They began to seal the hideout entrance. From there, more rocks plunged all the way to the canyon floor.

It was an avalanche!

I would find out later that fortunately, Uncle Steve and Katie were aware of the possibility of an avalanche and they had found a safe place to wait it out.

It took what seemed like forever for the rocks to stop sliding. It took even longer for the dust clouds to settle. Once the dust cleared, it was quite apparent that both caves were completely sealed.

Amy, Sarah, and Kai had raced to the back of the cave and had gotten out safely through the back exit before the explosion took place. They climbed up to the top of the mountain to find Rex and me standing in the field of yellow flowers. They rushed over and embraced us.

Amy informed us that Mr. Smith and Mr. Jones were still in the hideout. We told her that the front entrance was sealed but we knew they could exit through the rear entrance.

Amy didn't think they would be able to use any kind of exit for a long time. And quite frankly, she didn't think that anyone would want to go into that cave for quite a while. The two men were having major intestinal difficulties and that cave would need some major cleaning.

As for Woodrow and Calvin, I told Amy that if the dynamite hadn't gotten them, then the rockslide probably had. And if the rockslide hadn't gotten them, the front of the cave was sealed forever. But the rear exit was still open.

'Yes, there is an exit,' we were reminded by Rex, *'but they would have to pass by Claire and her cubs. The odds are not very good that they would be successful at doing that.'*

We knew that the two brothers would never bother us again.

I could see that Sarah was back to her old self. She had apparently eaten enough plants to rid herself of her sickness. We were relieved to see her doing so well.

We decided to leave the mountaintop and rest at the lions' cave for a while.

I contacted Uncle Steve via the two-way and told him that we were all fine and I congratulated him on still being the best shot in the county.

Amy got on the two-way and asked Uncle Steve if it would be OK with him if we took a few hours to talk to our new friends before going down to the canyon floor for dinner and camping there overnight. We would have the whole next day to get back to Mountview.

Uncle Steve was fine with that. He and Katie were shaken, but unscathed. This had been quite an ordeal for them as well. Uncle Steve was looking forward to another home-cooked meal from Katie. Apparently, she now could cook, she handled snakes, and she could speak Spanish. My little sister was really growing up.

Sarah sent, 'W*here do I begin? So much has happened since we last saw each other.'*

Rex nodded. *'There is some important information that you should know. Let's start there.'*

We sat down near the entrance to the cave with our backs resting against the cool rock face. The sun was out, the shade was comfortable, and there was enough light for us to see. Kai and Aiden, our new mountain lion best friends, lay down by the front of the cave to watch over us as we talked. Claire remained back in the shadows, guarding her babies. We didn't bother her.

Rex proceeded to send us a story. 'Schmooneys have been on this earth for a long, long, long time. While Schmooneys have much strength, we also have weaknesses. One of those weaknesses is that we, just like humans and other animals, can get sick. Unfortunately, we cannot go to doctors to get remedies; we must find our remedies like other animals and that is in the forests. The goldenseal plant is our remedy. It cures many of our illnesses, very similar to penicillin for humans.

'There are very few naturally growing fields of the goldenseal plant. Those fields are not located in an area convenient for Schmooneys from all over the world to travel to. Over the years, many Schmooneys died from their illnesses before they could reach the golden fields. We were losing our brothers and sisters at an alarming rate.

'So, a long, long, time ago The Lord of the Forest made twelve special birds to help us with this problem. He sent these twelve birds out in pairs to serve six of the seven continents. We knew that our plants could not live in Antarctica, so we didn't send a pair to that continent. With each pair, one bird carried the seeds of sustenance in his beak and the other bird carried the water of life. Their sole purpose was to carry these "seeds of life" to every continent and to provide enough water for the seeds to grow and flourish. We needed to provide fields of yellow flowers for our Schmooneys all over the world.

'On each continent, we were able to grow our seedlings, spread the flowers, and develop centers for life. Schmooneys throughout the world now find life in fields of flowers close to them. There they can fight off infection, rid themselves of disease, and find the warmth and comfort they need in order to energize themselves to go back and protect the animals in the forests all over the world.

'Each of these birds, called a Voltare, planted and watered the initial seedlings. Their memory continues to protect our gardens today. At each field, we have enlisted the help of those animals in the nearby forests to serve, protect, and spread our word so as to preserve what we have started. Just as we have done in this field.

'On each continent we have Schmooneys, just like you, Sarah, but each continent has a Schmooney that, in its natural state, looks different than Sarah. That is because each Schmooney is made up of the animals on that particular continent. So the South American Schmooney is made up of seven animals from South and Central America. The African

Schmooney is made up of seven animals from the African continent. This is because each Schmooney must be able to communicate with all the animals in their area, just like Sarah communicates with all the animals in the North America forests, but each continent has different animals. So each Schmooney looks different.'

'*I hope to be going to Costa Rica next summer. Will I be able to see a Schmooney there?*' I sent.

'*Well, you might,*' he replied. '*Now that you know what to look for, you can see Schmooneys on six continents, although each one will look different.*'

'*Oh, I can't wait,*' I sent.

Rex continued. '*At each field, we have protectors, which guard the fields against destruction. I have been chosen to protect this field and that is my lifetime project. Since the mountain lions have a home next to this field, it was natural for me to change into a mountain lion. But actually, I am a Schmooney.*

'*Schmooneys all over the world have been entrusted with the protection of their fields. They, just like me, can never leave their appointed duty. If something happens to this crop, then our existence is at risk. We cannot risk letting this crop be destroyed. Schmooneys that eat these leaves and plants every day can live forever, for they provide our lifeblood. Then we can continue to carry on our work and keep our animals healthy.*'

'*So what is a Voltare? Have I ever seen one?*' I sent.

'*A Voltare is a bird of unique design. Remember, Sarah is a North American Schmooney and she is made of seven different animals. Each and every Schmooney is made of seven different animals from their assigned continent. The Voltare is made of seven different birds. The Voltare is a unique bird and it still lives today. But since their duty has been fulfilled, they rarely come out from their homes. However, if we ever need them again, they will be there for us.*'

'*What seven birds is the Voltare made of?*' I asked.

'*Each letter of its name represents one of the animals that comprise the Voltare: vulture, ostrich, loon, tern, albatross, raven, and the eagle. Since life is all about communing and sharing gifts and strengths, their combined gifts gave us a bird capable of withstanding all the natural* elements. By combining the strengths of these birds, The Lord of the Forest made certain that the Voltare would accomplish its appointed task of building fields all over the world. We now have fields located on every continent.'

Sarah sent, *'So, where is Stuart, Grandfather?'*

'Your brother was needed elsewhere and was sent to South America to help protect the animals in the rainforest. You were very young when our family came here. This field was destroyed many, many years ago. Shortly after the field was destroyed, we lost your mother and father, because there weren't any goldenseal plants nearby to save them from disease. The Lord of the Forest sent the Voltare to bring back seeds and leaves; however, it was too late for your parents. I was needed to protect this field so I stayed here, where I will now remain. You and your brother were saved and you traveled back to your forest to accomplish your task, to protect the forests in your area. Stuart was sent to South America.'

'Are there really Schmooneys all over the world?' I sent.

'Yes,' Rex replied. *'I have not been to the other continents, but I know this is true. And I have seen Sarah's brother. Stuart is a fine looking Schmooney. I believe that you three will meet someday. But I do not know when that will be.'*

Rex paused a moment as if to make certain he had answered our questions.

He continued, *'Now I want to make a few points and ask some questions. Sarah, you are young, healthy, and growing in knowledge. I will always be here, so come back when you can. We can talk and I will share my knowledge with you.'* Rex moved closer to Sarah. *'But you must return home now. You have been away from your duties too long. You have a forest to protect and the lives of many animals are your responsibility.'* He reached out his paw and touched Sarah's back. *'I am very proud of you.'*

Sarah moved closer to Rex and rubbed her head against his side. It was just like my parents reaching out to touch me or pat my shoulder. Really cool!

Rex looked over at me. He sent to Sarah, *'Now tell me about Austin. How does Austin have the ability to hear us? I have heard that there were humans that could send, but I have never met one. When he first sent me a message, I was amazed. I had to sit down and figure out what was happening.'* Without waiting for Sarah's reply, he turned to me. *'So, Austin is your gift the ability to send?'*

'Yes, sir,' I responded. *'I have the gift of communicating without speaking. Dr. Dixon calls it telepathy.'*

'I have heard of humans sending. You are a very brave young man, Austin. Didn't I scare you when your first saw me?'

'Yes, sir, you scared me plenty,' I answered truthfully. *'But Sarah is my friend and she needed our help. I didn't have time to be real scared.'*

Rex nodded that he understood. *'You have very good friends, Sarah. Good friends are very important and you seem to have quite a few of them. You and your friends are welcome here anytime.*

'I would ask that you send me a message before you come, but there are limits to sending. Some of the masters can send over long distances, but most Schmooneys, including me, can only send within their own domain.

'So when you come, send to me from the bottom of this canyon. Then I will make sure of your safety.' Rex continued.

Sarah agreed. *'Austin's gift seems to be growing. He may help us extend our sending range. We will come visit you, Grandfather.'*

'Now you know how the fields have been planted throughout the world. You know that there are Schmooneys on every continent. You know where your brother is. And you know that your grandfather loves you very much and will always be here for you. So, Sarah, go share your gift. Help those that need your help and learn from those who will help you grow. Austin is a great friend.' Rex looked over at me. *'Keep him close to you.'*

Rex scanned the area. Satisfied that we were all safe he sent, *'I will be going now. I have a field to protect and friends that need to be fed. Remember, always be sure to use your gifts and share them. I love you.'* He rose from the ground. He stretched for a moment and sniffed the air. Then he stroked Sarah's back and rubbed against her. He came over and rubbed against me, then stood still for a moment, sniffing the air once more.

Kai and Aidan were now standing up and ready to move once Rex was ready.

Before I could blink, the three of them disappeared into the cave.

Chapter 18

We scaled the wall and returned to the canyon floor. We were totally exhausted, but felt much better when Uncle Steve and Katie greeted us enthusiastically. Katie had prepared dinner. I must say, it was really good - or maybe I was just really hungry. I don't know which, but it really didn't matter. The fact was that I don't believe bacon and eggs have ever tasted better.

We shared our stories and talked well into the night. Uncle Steve's ankle was much better. The advice that Amy had given him had worked. Sarah felt like her old self again. She had taken a bag of leaves and berries with her, just in case. Amy and I had some cuts and bruises, but nothing too serious. Although we were very excited to see each other, after our delicious meal and some heavy discussions, we fell soundly to sleep.

I had the feeling that, although I couldn't see them, we were being watched and protected by our new mountain lion friends.

The next morning, none of us wanted to get up. We were sore, tired, and not looking forward to our trek back to the Suburban. However, after a quick breakfast, we were up and hiking back through the path that had brought us here. Not a lot was said. Not even a complaint.

Fortunately, it was a non-eventful hike to the Suburban and, from there, home. We had had enough excitement to last a lifetime.

Once we were home, we didn't want to move. Honestly. Amy had assigned some of her staff, which included Christina, to take care of the animals while we were gone. Everything was fine at the Center. The staff agreed to take care of the animals for another day without us. We were extremely grateful for one day of rest!

Katie and I were still sore and tired. Since we had the day off, we planned to sleep in and eat just about everything in the refrigerator. Dad called while we were at Uncle Steve's that day and we shared most of what had happened.

Of course, there were some things that we didn't share. It wasn't that we weren't telling the truth; it was just not necessary to worry anyone. Dad was fine since he knew that Uncle Steve and Amy were with us. He always wanted to make certain that we were safe and protected. We assured him that we were.

Immediately upon returning, Uncle Steve had contacted the authorities to file a report. The police were looking into the matter. Uncle Steve and Amy had to fill out several lengthy reports and wade through a bunch of criminal photographs to see if they could identify any of the people we had seen up there. They couldn't. Uncle Steve made certain to tell the sheriff that there were mountain lions at the site and they shouldn't be disturbed. The sheriff understood what he meant and Uncle Steve was satisfied that our new friends would not be bothered. There was no need to mention the gold. After all, none of us had actually seen any.

Amy contacted the Western North Carolina Nature Center and advised Mr. Baker that there were mountain lions living in that area. Mr. Baker was thrilled to hear that news and promised to contact the proper agencies. Mr. Baker also understood that those mountain lions should not be disturbed. So the information that Amy shared was classified as 'confidential' and was limited to only a few trusted employees.

Amy had also called Dr. Dixon when we returned and he was thrilled that Sarah was healthy. She asked if he would mind dropping by the Nature Center the following day so we could give him all the details, which were plentiful. He wanted to come over immediately, but agreed to be patient.

The next day, Katie and I were back at work at the Nature Center when I saw Dr. Dixon arrive. Before he could say anything, I blurted out, "What an adventure!" and proceeded to fill him in on several of the really cool things that happened. "I can't wait for next year. We have so much to do."

We went inside and sat down in Amy's office. I thought Amy's office was cool since it was filled with lots of books and posters of different animals and she had an awesome collection of frog statues. I'm not kidding – there were frogs everywhere, but they weren't real. She had copper frogs playing banjos, marble frogs on lily pads, wire frogs catching flies with their tongues. I was sure one day I'd walk in and find a picture of frogs playing poker!

Katie, Amy (who was holding and petting Sarah), and I told Dr. Dixon everything that happened. We were so wound up that Dr. Dixon had to ask us to slow down several times. He took notes as we spoke and it was obvious that he was completely amazed at our adventure. We talked so long that Amy had to call Uncle Steve and ask him to bring sandwiches out to the Center for us.

We ate throughout our discussion. Katie, Uncle Steve, Amy, Sarah and I had just experienced an incredible adventure. "A lifetime adventure," as Dr. Dixon said. He took so many notes, his pen ran out of ink. He couldn't write fast enough. Amy gave him a new pen from her frog pencil holder.

Finally, we finished our stories. Dr. Dixon put down his new pen and shook his head. "What an adventure you all have had!"

"Yes, sir, it's too bad that we don't have anything to show for it," I said ruefully.

"What do you mean, Austin?' Amy asked.

"Well, you know, we were so close to that gold statue, and no one will ever know it, will they? Can we go back and dig out the gold some day?" I asked.

"Well, we could go back and try," Amy responded. "But none of us ever saw the statue, did we? We just took their word for it. It could have been a big statue or maybe it was just a small statue. We'll never know. Plus, it's now buried under so much rock and stone that no one will ever see that statue again. It's forever sealed in the cave." She paused. "And really, Austin, you didn't do all that for the gold, did you?"

"No," I replied. "No, we didn't do it for the gold."

Uncle Steve nodded. "I know what you're saying. You aren't interested in the gold, you're interested in showing someone that we were actually there and that the Golden Gato is real."

"Yes, that's exactly right," I agreed.

"Wouldn't it be neat if we did find some real gold?" Katie chimed in.

"But we *do* know it's real. Don't we?" prodded Uncle Steve.

"Those men sure thought so," Amy concurred.

"Yes, I do know it's real," I said. "But that's not the point. I was there. Well, I didn't really see it, but I was there. But it would be cool to have something to remember this adventure."

Amy stood up. "Well, maybe there is something that I could do that would prove that we were there and that there was actually gold there."

"What?" Uncle Steve asked.

"Yeah, what do you mean?" I wondered.

Amy reached into her pocket and removed something that was wrapped in a piece of cloth. "Well, it seems that things got really busy in the hideout, there at the end. Those two poor souls, Mr. Jones and Mr. Smith, were in no condition to prevent me from 'borrowing' something from them. And, actually, it was Woodrow who gave me the idea. See, when Woodrow was packing his bag, he overlooked one item. That's what kept him there so long; he couldn't find it. He couldn't find the wrapped item that I have right here. I'm sure that Calvin specifically instructed him to take this with him." She paused.

Sarah sent a message, *'I know what it is.'*

I said out loud, "Sarah knows what it is but I don't. What is it?"

Amy revealed her prize as she slowly pulled off the last piece of cloth – it was a large chunk of gold!

It was about six inches long and two inches wide. The light streaming through the window seemed to light it up from inside.

Dr. Dixon gasped. "Oh my!"

"Ohhhhh," Katie murmured.

My mouth dropped open.

Uncle Steve smiled affectionately. "Why you..." Then he squeezed Amy's shoulder.

Amy grinned proudly. "Apparently, one of the men knocked a piece of gold off of the statue. I had seen it the night when it was Calvin's turn to stay awake for his watch. I was trying to escape, so I didn't sleep much. I happened to notice him carefully unwrapping this little package so he could stare at it. Apparently, he thought everyone was asleep. But I wasn't. It was actually kind of creepy, the way he was so obsessed with it. I watched him hide it and grabbed it the next day when I had the chance."

"I wonder if it is cursed," I said.

"Well, in Calvin's case, it **was** cursed. Look what happened to him, " Uncle Steve pointed out.

'Do you think it's cursed?' I sent to Sarah.

Sarah sent, *'Not anymore. This is your souvenir. Keep it and it will never curse you. However, if you let the gold take over your life, then you will be cursed.'*

"Let's just keep this to ourselves," Amy suggested. "We'll put it in the library at Uncle Steve's place and it will always remind us of our adventure. It will represent our 'golden rule' on how to treat people."

We passed the gold chunk around so that each of us got to hold it. I was surprised to find how heavy such a small piece of gold actually felt.

"Well, life in Mountview was never this exciting until you three arrived," Dr. Dixon commented, looking at Katie and me, then patting Sarah. "I know that summer is just about over, and I will really miss you two." Dr. Dixon held out his arms and Katie and I gave him a big hug.

"We'll miss you, too, Dr. Dixon," we both said.

"And you'll be back next summer," Uncle Steve interjected. "I have already cleared it with your mom. She called this morning and I told her we were all just fine and that Mountview couldn't survive a summer without you two."

"All right!" I exclaimed.

"That means both you **and** Katie will be coming," Amy added, waiting to see how I would react.

I looked at Katie. "That's fine with me. She's not so bad for a kid sister." I patted her shoulder.

"You're not so bad for a big brother," Katie added, patting me in return.

"Speaking of which, I've got some work to finish before dinner," Uncle Steve said. "We need to get home and get you two packed tonight. Your parents are picking you up tomorrow morning."

"Where has the summer gone?" Amy wondered. "It went by so fast. Katie, will you help me with Sarah's cage? I need to clean it and move it to the back room."

"Sure," Katie replied, jumping to her feet.

"Then we'll all go back to the house for dinner. Dr. Dixon, can you join us?" Amy asked.

"Oh no, but thank you," Dr. Dixon responded.

Amy stood up, holding Sarah. She followed Katie and Uncle Steve as they left the room.

Dr. Dixon looked at me. "So, what will you do? I guess you'll go to school and learn your ABC's."

"Yes, sir," I replied. "I'll do my schoolwork and I'll also learn more about my gift and practice using it. I'll also do a lot of reading. And I'll be thinking about Sarah and Mountview and all of you."

"Yes, those are all good things to do. Now, if you promise to do really well in school and practice your gift, I have one more thing to add to your schedule," Dr. Dixon said. "I have been talking with my friends regarding my trip to Costa Rica next summer." He was looking at me closely. I could sense something was coming.

He continued. "They have advised me that if I want to bring an associate with me and Mrs. Dixon, they will approve. What that means, young Austin, is, would you like to go visit a real rainforest in Costa Rica next summer?"

"Would I? Totally right, I would!" I exclaimed. Then I thought it through. "But I'll need my parents' permission, won't I?"

"Yes, you will, but I'm pretty certain that they will let you go," he said reassuringly. "Let me show you a picture of the city where we will be staying. Actually, the picture is more of the hotel where we will be staying." Dr. Dixon checked his pockets for the picture. "One of my associates took the picture and sent it to me. I have it right here... now, what did I do with it? Oh yes, here it is." He pulled out a picture of the hotel and showed it to me.

There was the hotel - a tall, white, modern building of at least twenty stories. The grass was lush and the trees were tall and leafy, just like you would expect. There were jagged mountains as a backdrop, fading into a clear blue sky. It created an awesome picture.

A parking lot wound around the right side of the building, which led to another building. When I looked at the top of that building, there were several additional mountain peaks behind it that seemed to touch the blue sky.

But there was something odd about one of the mountains. I took a closer look.

"Anything wrong, Austin?" Dr. Dixon asked.

"No, sir. Nothing wrong, but look at this one mountain back here." I pointed to the picture. "Does this mountain look different to you?"

Dr. Dixon took the photograph and studied it. He used his bifocals, which meant he had to raise his head up a little to get a more precise look. "Ah, I see what you are saying. This one mountain back here looks a bit different than the others, doesn't it? It seems to be a bit flatter than the others. And, ah yes, it seems to have a gold cap on the top of it. I wonder what that means?"

"May I see it again, please?" I requested.

Dr. Dixon handed the photograph back to me and I studied it closely. "Yes, sir. I believe you are exactly right. That *is* a golden field on top of that mountain."

"Austin, are you thinking what I'm thinking?" Dr. Dixon asked excitedly.

I put the picture down and looked at Dr. Dixon. "Yes, sir. I believe we are thinking the very same thing. A golden field on top of a flat mountain means only one thing to me. I believe a Voltare has been there. Next summer we may get to see a South American Schmooney."

"Yes, I believe we will, young man," Dr. Dixon smiled. "So, what do you say to that?"

"I say, I can't wait until next summer!"

About The Author

Bob Shumaker was raised in Cuyahoga Falls, Ohio and now lives in Simpsonville, South Carolina with his wife, Sharon and their daughter, Katy. He retired early from his sales and marketing company to focus on one of his lifelong passions: writing. He began writing at age nine, inventing short stories and plays for his family and friends, and has never lost his love of storytelling. *The Curse of the Golden Gato* is Book Three of The Schmooney Trilogies, a series of fantasy adventure novels for children and young adults. Book One, *The Secret of the Enchanted Forest*, Book Two, *The Spirit of the Turquoise Necklace* and the picture book, *The Legend of The Schmooney,* are available at leading book sellers. Watch the website www.schmooney.com for news about his next books and other creative ventures.

Printed in the United States
80990LV00003B/139-249